PRAISE FOR
The Quest of the Warrior Sheep

"Hilarious crime caper involving a gang of sheep and a mobile phone...what more could you ask for?"

—*Books Monthly*

"The most unlikely of all epic adventure novels you will ever come across."

—James, *Kid's Compass*

"I loved this book from the first chapter to the last."

—*The Bookbag*

"In a series launch, this husband-and-wife team sends a quirky group of characters careening across England at a madcap pace...It's all about the journey: barnyard puns (including a llama lama who speaks in parables) and the running conceit of the herd's unusual intelligence, despite their share of woolly headed moments, will go a long way in keeping middle grade readers engaged."

—*Publishers Weekly*

"The first adventure (with another on the way) of the Warrior Sheep by the British husband-and-wife pair is planted firmly in *Wallace & Gromit* country. Young fans of deadpan Brit humor will enjoy this fleecy romp."

—*Kirkus*

"The rapid pacing of *The Quest of the Warrior Sheep*, snappy dialogue, and outrageously funny British humor made this a hit with my students...I thoroughly enjoyed *The Quest of the Warrior Sheep* and read it in one sitting."

—*School Library Journal* blog *Practically Paradise*

PRAISE FOR
The Warrior Sheep Go West

"Readers will be laughing out loud as they follow this comedy adventure full of twists, surprises, and a happy ending."

—*Library Media Connection*

"The adventurous episodes keep things moving along, while the hilarity takes hold."

—*School Library Journal*

"The Russells, a British husband-and-wife writing team, trot out their brave-but-foolish fleecy heroes for another preposterous romp full of wild coincidences, evil scientists, mad magicians, and enough misunderstandings for three novels."

—*Kirkus*

The Warrior

SHEEP Down Under

CHRISTINE & CHRISTOPHER RUSSELL

sourcebooks
jabberwocky

Text copyright © Christopher and Christine Russell 2012
Cover illustration copyright © Colin Stimpson 2012
The authors and cover illustrator have asserted their moral rights.
Cover and internal design © 2012 by Sourcebooks, Inc.
Sourcebooks and the colophon are registered trademarks of
Sourcebooks, Inc.

The characters and events portrayed in this book are fictitious
or are used fictitiously. Any similarity to real persons, living or
dead, is purely coincidental and not intended by the author.

Published by Sourcebooks Jabberwocky, an imprint of Sourcebooks,
Inc.
P.O. Box 4410, Naperville, Illinois 60567-4410
(630) 961-3900
Fax: (630) 961-2168
www.jabberwockykids.com

First published 2012 in the United Kingdom under the title
The Warrior Sheep Down Under by Egmont UK Limited, 239
Kensington High Street, London W8 6SA.

Library of Congress Cataloging-in-Publication data is on file with
the publisher.

Source of Production: Versa Press, East Peoria, Illinois, USA
Date of Production: January 2012
Run Number: 16779

Printed and bound in the United States of America.
VP 10 9 8 7 6 5 4 3 2 1

This book is dedicated to Rachel Boden,
first champion of the Warrior Sheep.

Contents

1
The Sound of Destiny

There it goes again."

The sheep all listened. It was a sound that was beginning to worry them. A kind of sobbing and sighing and tapping all in one.

"It's the sea, man," said Links, the Lincoln Longwool.

"No, it isn't," said Jaycey, the pretty little Jacob. "The sea goes *whoosh, splash, whoosh.*"

"My stomachs are going *gurgle, gurgle, gurgle,*" complained Oxo, the large Oxford ram. "When's that Rose going to bring our lunch?"

"We've only just had breakfast, dear," pointed out Sal, the Southdown ewe. "She gave us cauliflowers, remember? Just like home."

Home. For a moment they all paused and stared at the grass beneath their hooves. It was two days now since they'd left their home at Eppingham Farm. Not that they were particularly worried about being away.

They were, after all, no ordinary ovines. They were Ida White's rare breeds flock. They were the Eppingham Five. The Warrior Sheep. In fact, they had all been excited when Ida told them they were to have a vacation at the seaside. It would be a little adventure. Nothing like the grand adventures that had taken them to the North and the West, but a bit of a change while Ida and her grandson Tod were in Australia, visiting Ida's brother, Frank.

Ida had explained that Australia was a long way away and, much as she would like to, she couldn't afford to take them with her. So that was all right and, at first, the sheep had liked Murkton-on-Sea. It was very nice in its seasidey way. And Ida's sister, Rose, who was looking after them, was perfectly nice too. And so was the field and the grazing and the hut in the corner where they sheltered from the wind. Everything was perfectly nice. Except for that sound.

"It's nothing to worry about," said Wills, the Balwen Welsh lamb. He was standing a little away from the rest, gazing down at the harbor below. "It's just the wind. When it blows through the rigging of the yachts down there it makes those weird noises."

A breeze wafted sea mist up toward them and the sound grew stronger.

Links tossed his curls. "Respect," he said. "Wills, you is probably right but, man, that noise is gettin' on my nerves." He raised and nodded his woolly head, then began to rap.

"We's real turned off by this seaside ting,
It's maybe OK if you's a bird on the wing,
But we is sheep, and we can only rap,
And it ain't no use against the sob, sigh, and tap.
You hear what I'm sayin: the sob, sigh, and tap?
It's drivin' me crazy, so give me a map,
An' help me escape from the land of the haddock,
Way back inland to my Eppingham paddock..."

Links was pleased with "haddock." He didn't actually know what a haddock *was*, but he'd heard the word recently and it was a great rhyme for "paddock."

Still nodding, he turned to see if the others were about to join in with his rap but the grass between him and the hut was now empty of sheep. Oxo's broad head appeared in the hut doorway.

"You'd better come in, mate," he called. "Sal's being inspired."

While Links ambled toward the hut, Sal's inspiration was turning to irritation.

"Yachts in the harbor, is it?" she scoffed at Wills. "The ropes and wires and the masts and things?"

Wills nodded, suddenly afraid to say more. Not only was he the youngest of the Eppingham Five, he was also an orphan and had had no mother to teach him the ways of sheep. Instead, he'd been brought up in Ida White's farmhouse kitchen, along with her grandson, Tod. Because of this start in life, he knew something of human ways, which had proved very useful at times, but such knowledge had never impressed Sal. She saw it as her task to impart sheepliness to the skinny lamb in front of her. To educate Wills. The others needed her guidance too, of course. Constantly. But Wills needed it most because of his very unsheeply habit of thinking for himself. That was what he was doing now, and doing it while Sal was being inspired.

Links squeezed into the hut. The breeze and the weird, worrying sound wafted in after him. Sal turned and stood with her head to one side, listening. She

4

could hear the sounds of *Despair*. Of someone Trapped.
Helpless. Sorrowful. In Danger. Tap, tap, tapping in the
Forlorn Hope of Rescue...She turned again to Wills,
who was shifting uncomfortably from hoof to hoof, his
eyes fixed on the floor.

"You may, just possibly, be right," she said.

Wills looked up, surprised.

"*Whereas*," continued Sal, glaring at him, "the Songs
of the Fleece are *never* wrong."

She swiftly turned her yellow-eyed glare on the
others, cutting short their collective groan. "Were they
wrong about Lambad the Bad?" she demanded. "No!
We listened to the prophetic verses and we traveled
North to *vanquish* Lambad. Were they wrong about
Red Tongue? No! We listened again and went West to
destroy the evil monster Red Tongue. Twice we have listened and twice we have saved sheepdom from slavery
and extinction. The Songs of the Fleece were not wrong
then. So why should they be wrong about Tuftella?"

"*Tuftella?*" the other sheep inquired loudly as one.
Even Wills.

Sal regarded them as if they were a lost cause. "Yes,
Tuftella. The fairest ewe of all."

5

Jaycey pouted but said nothing.

Sal closed her eyes and began to recite.

"Tuftella, fairest ewe of all,

One day will into danger fall.

Where once she grazed on mountains high,

Her fleece the finest 'neath the sky,

Her ears, her hooves the daintiest yet,

That caused to swoon each ram she met,

Alas, alack, the time will come

When she is hidden from the sun,

And locked in darkest tower tall

Whilst 'neath her snapping monsters crawl.

A sheeply maiden in distress…"

"What's a maiden?" interrupted Oxo, his voice low and serious this time.

"A young female," whispered Wills. "Like Jaycey."

Oxo glanced at Jaycey. "Is *she* in distress then?"

"Only when her fleece goes frizzy in the rain," murmured Wills with a giggle. "Distress means trouble."

"When you've all quite finished!" said Sal without opening her eyes. She waited for silence then resumed.

"A sheeply maiden in distress,

How sharply will her troubles press.

Her plaintive cries will waft and float

Across the sea to shores remote.

But who will heed them, who will ride

To break her free, to take her side?

Who will face the final thunder,

And lift Tuftella from Down Under?"

Nobody spoke. Then, eventually:

"Um. *Us?*" ventured Wills.

"Of course it's us!" cried Sal. "It can only be us. We're the Warrior Sheep!"

"Too right, man," agreed Links. "Let's get rescuin'!"

"Yeah! Bring on the snapping monsters!" roared Oxo, pawing the ground and eyeballing the nearest doorpost.

Only Jaycey was unmoved by the tidal wave of enthusiasm. She hadn't at all liked the "fairest ewe" bit. Or the line about Tuftella's fleece being the "finest." Or her ears and hooves the "daintiest." The Songs of the Fleece were so last year and garbage. If there was any swooning to be done, whatever *that* was, rams with decent eyesight should be doing it at Jaycey's feet, not tacky Tuftella's. What a stupid name anyway.

"And where's this Down Under?" she asked sniffily. "If it's farther than North or West, you can forget it."

The question produced instant silence. Only Wills ever knew the answer to this kind of thing. All eyes turned to him.

"Um. Australia, I think. And maybe New Zealand too."

"Australia!" Sal's gasp caused the little hut to wobble. "Isn't that where Tod and Ida have gone? A very, *very* long way away?"

Wills nodded. "On the other side of the world."

"That's that then," said Jaycey, flouncing past the others and out into the field. "Tuftella will just have to save her own fly-bitten fleece."

The others followed her out. The breeze was stronger now and the sound of sighing and sobbing filled their heads. Even Jaycey began to feel a bit ashamed of herself.

Wills still felt sure it was the wind in the boats' rigging. And yet...It also *did* sound like someone crying and calling for help. And as Sal had pointed out, the prophetic verses had never been wrong. Wills turned suddenly, wriggled under the fence, and trotted quickly away down the winding lane to the sea. The others followed, not knowing why, but somehow drawn toward the sad sound calling to them. Calling from across the water.

They stopped on the harbor wall, behind a pile of lobster pots, and stared hopelessly at the waves. Somewhere out there was Down Under. But how could they possibly cross this mighty ocean?

Then Wills's eyes were drawn to the bulk of a large boat moored in the harbor. Tethered to the wall. Tethered like a sleek, powerful animal. Wills had never seen such a vessel, even on television in the farmhouse kitchen. He could tell it was fast: its twin hulls seemed to lean forward eagerly and when the engines suddenly started, their roar and rumble scared and thrilled him in equal measure. He crept nearer still and saw the name painted on the boat's hull: DESTINY.

Crew members were hurrying to and fro, loading supplies from vans parked on the quayside.

"What's the panic, Skip?" panted one of the men as he shouldered a box labeled *Very Expensive Cosmetics*.

"The owner just phoned," replied the skipper.

"She'll be here in half an hour. And she doesn't take kindly to being kept waiting."

"She must be mega rich to own a boat like this!" called one of the van drivers. The skipper didn't reply. The van driver called again. "So where you headed?"

"New Zealand," grunted the skipper.

"What, all the way Down Under?"

"Yep. Not bad for a maiden voyage, eh?"

• • •

On the harbor wall, Wills stood frozen. But his head was spinning. He heard himself mumbling.

"Destiny...Down Under...Down Under...Maiden Voyage...Maiden...Maiden in Distress...Sheeply Maiden in Distress. DOWN UNDER...MAIDEN IN DISTRESS... DESTINY...MAIDEN VOYAGE!"

He steadied himself. The others were staring at him, openmouthed.

"Quick," Wills breathed. "We've got a boat to catch!"

2
Sheep Ahoy

W hat the heck are *they*?"

"Sheep, Skip," replied the deckhand.

They were indeed sheep. Five of them. Standing at the top of the gangway, blinking at the two men.

"Where did they come from?"

The deckhand shrugged. "One of the vans, I s'pose. I'll ask the drivers when they get back from coffee."

The skipper glanced irritably at his watch. "No. Just get rid of them."

"What if they're her pets?" asked the deckhand helpfully.

"She never said anything about bringing sheep!"

"She never said anything about bringing her own chef," replied the deckhand. "And he's already in the galley slicing up mangoes."

"Yes, all right, all right." The skipper gestured sharply.

The sheep saw and nipped quickly aboard.

"Put them in hold number one," said the skipper.

"Can't," said the deckhand. "Her multigym's in there. I could make them a pen under the life rafts?"

"OK." The skipper, Ed, blew a sigh. He had a feeling that the next few weeks wouldn't be all plain sailing.

"Captain Ted, I presume. Lovely to meet you."

The owner had breezed on-board. A shortish, plump woman swathed in pink trousers and a silky tunic. Expensive perfume filled the air. Ed gulped in several hundred dollars' worth as he turned to face the pearly toothed smile, the flawless complexion, the neat plum-colored hair of Alice Barton.

"It's, um, Ed, ma'am, not Ted—"

"Oh, do forgive me." She was wrinkling her smoothly powdered nose. "There's an ambience, Ted," she purred. "Do something about it, will you?"

The skipper stared at her. If by ambience she meant a smell, then of course there was an *ambience*. She'd brought a bunch of sheep on-board. He bit his tongue and said nothing. Alice swept on past and Ed noticed behind her a skinny, pale young woman stumbling down the gangway, bent double under the weight of a huge rucksack marked *Laptops and Other Important Stuff*.

"Where shall I set up the office, Miss Barton?" she gasped.

"In my room, dear," said Alice over her shoulder.

"Cabin," corrected Ed, then wished he hadn't. Alice turned, her beaming smile frozen.

"My *room*, Ted," she said. "On *my* boat. Do we understand each other?"

Ed shrugged and nodded. "I think we're beginning to," he said.

Alice's smile returned to full brightness. "That's all right then. Do get a move on, Deidre, poppet. I've got phone calls to make."

Deidre, who was Alice Barton's new personal assistant, gave Ed a nervous little smile as she struggled past with her load.

• • •

By now, the sheep had been penned in a little space under the life rafts. They could no longer hear the plaintive cries and tap, tap, tapping of the maiden in distress, only the low throb of the idling engines and the hiss of white water around the stern of the boat.

Wills was trying to explain. "One of those men said this boat's going on her *maiden* voyage," he whispered.

Links nodded. "'Nuff said."

Wills hoped so. "And there's another thing. The boat's called *Destiny*."

The others stared at him blankly.

"Destiny's something that's *meant* to happen."

"What, like supper?" asked Oxo.

"More important than supper," said Wills. Then he added quickly, before Oxo could ask, "More important than breakfast too. Something *really* important. Something like having to rescue a maiden in distress."

Sal had caught on and, raising her head, she suddenly bleated loudly, "We are coming, Tuftella. It is our Destiny!"

The sheep huddled together, staring toward the endless sea, suddenly rather scared. Could it really be that the future was not entirely in their own hooves? That Destiny might be guiding them? Perhaps it always was.

They became aware that the other *Destiny*, the boat guided by Skipper Ed, was now moving. She'd been untied and was gliding gracefully out of the harbor. When she was clear, her engines surged to full speed, and for some time the sheep could only brace themselves against the wind and spray, and watch the little town of Murkton dwindle behind them. Finally, when *Destiny* was well out to sea, Ed slowed to cruising speed. The engine noise softened again and the wind and spray eased.

"Ohmygrass..." Jaycey shook her pretty head. "What a relief. I can hear myself think again."

"Don't worry," grunted Oxo. "It won't deafen you."

Jaycey gave him a look, then turned to Wills. "Correct me if I'm wrong," she said, "but we're on this boat because *some* of us think a maiden in distress called to us. Right?"

Wills nodded warily. He knew what she was going to say next.

"So," continued Jaycey, fiercely, "if she's in that much distress, why can't we still hear her sobbing and sighing and tap, tap, tapping?"

Wills was actually wondering the same thing. He was also thinking back to the wind in the rigging of the yachts in the harbor. He was beginning to fear he'd made a truly dreadful mistake. But as he opened his mouth to admit it, Sal spoke.

"It's because of the sea air, dear," she said,

nodding wisely. "The salt gets in your ears and makes them go a bit funny. My aunt Sybil told me that, when I was a lamb—"

"Yeah, and my stomachs have gone a bit funny too," said Oxo. "I'm starving."

There was a moment's silence as the others realized they were too.

"Ohmygrass…" whimpered Jaycey, looking about at the bare wooden planks. "Ohmygrass…There *isn't* any grass."

But Oxo's nose was twitching. "Stick with me, kid," he said to Jaycey. "You'll be all right."

He ducked under the rope the deckhand had put up to keep them in, and trotted off. Quickly, the other warriors followed. Oxo's nose led him to a cabin in the middle of the boat. The sheep crowded around the partly open door and peered in.

Alice Barton was seated at her dressing table. Her short legs only just touched the ground and her rather fat bottom sagged on either side of the elegant little stool. She was surrounded by expensive skin creams and makeup and perfumes in little jars and bottles. She was mixing little dabs of this with little dabs of that.

Eventually, she smeared a little cream on her slightly puffy face.

"Ah, that is so good…" she murmured, gazing at herself in the mirror. "Alice, you must never neglect the face beautiful."

She took a slice of mango from the large plate of chopped fruit beside her. Oxo's nose was twitching violently now but Wills held him back.

"Not yet," he whispered.

"Excuse me, Miss Barton." An adjoining door opened and Deidre tiptoed into Alice's cabin.

"What is it, poppet?" sighed Alice, turning from the mirror.

"A phone call from someone who won't speak to me. Says it's private and he must talk to you personally. About Maiden Tower?"

Alice's eyebrows hit her plummy bangs. Wills's eyes opened wide too.

"I'll take it next door," Alice said. She took the phone Deidre was holding and marched briskly into the adjoining room. "Do go and get me some iced tea, angel."

"Yes, Miss Bart…" The door slammed in Deidre's face.

Wills and Oxo pressed themselves flat against the

wall outside the cabin as Deidre came out on deck, but she turned the other way.

Wills's brain was racing again. The Alice woman was at this very moment talking to someone about a place called Maiden Tower. Could this be the tower where Tuftella, the maiden in distress, was locked? And if so, why would a human know anything about it?

Oxo's mind was still on his stomachs. As soon as Deidre had gone, he was back in the doorway. This time he just couldn't wait. He barged in, snaffled up a mouthful of mango from the plate, and began to chew noisily. Jaycey followed him into the cabin, sprang on to the dressing table, and gazed at herself in the mirror.

"What shall I try first?" she asked excitedly, sniffing the perfumed air.

"Get down!" called Wills, as loudly as he dared.

Just then the plate of fruit slid from under Oxo's nose and crashed to the cabin floor.

"Ohmygrass..." bleated Jaycey. "Ohmygrass!" She turned quickly, trod in one of the little pots of greasy skin cream, skidded, and fell to the floor, followed by a shower of pots and bottles and jars. Their contents splashed and spilled in all directions.

18

"Deidre?" yelled Alice from the adjoining cabin. "What's going on in there?"

Led by Oxo, the warriors turned tail and ran out, skittering across the messy floor. They charged back toward the little roped-off area under the life rafts, all of them slipping and sliding on their greasy hooves.

Alice burst into her cabin, surveyed the mess for a moment, then strode out on to the deck, colliding with Deidre, who'd responded to her call. Deidre peered in, shocked.

"It wasn't me, Miss Barton. Honestly it wasn't."

Alice pushed her aside and began to follow the trail of lotions and potions. "Then we shall find out who it *was*, shan't we…"

Back in their little pen at the stern, the warriors huddled close together.

"I only wanted to try some perfume," whimpered Jaycey.

"Quite nice stuff this," mumbled Oxo through a mouthful of face cream. "Dunno what it is but it's all right…"

Links was looking at a trembling Wills. "What you tinking now, man?" he whispered. "You's 'bout to explode."

"Didn'tyouhear?" breathed Wills. "MaidenTower…She

was mixing up lotions and potions and she knows about a Maiden Tower…"

"Mm…" said Oxo, licking off the last of his face cream. "Lotions and potions, eh? Must remember that—"

"Listen," hissed Wills excitedly. "When I was in the farmhouse, Tod had a book about knights. Knights were sort of warriors. Like us? Only in the olden days."

Sal started listening. She was interested in the olden days. Even human olden days.

"And these knights," said Wills, "went about doing good deeds. Like rescuing maidens in distress."

"What, even tacky ones?" asked Jaycey.

"Yes! And here's the strange thing. *Sometimes* they had help from a lady. I think Tod called her a fairy god-mother. Anyway, this lady always had lots of special lotions and potions she mixed together to make things happen to other people."

"Ohmygrass…" Jaycey's eyes stretched wide. "You think the Alice woman is a fairy whatdidyoucallit, then?"

Wills shrugged. "Yes—maybe."

"Ohmygrass…" repeated Jaycey. "You don't…you don't think she'll be angry and make something happen to *me*, do you, Wills? She won't make me *ugly*?"

"No, Jaycey," said Wills. "That's the whole point. If we're right about her, she'll be on *our* side!"

But as he spoke, a shadow fell across the sheep. Alice Barton was looming above them.

She stared silently down, but then turned abruptly and strode away. Ed the skipper had heard the earlier commotion and was coming down the steps from the bridge. Alice barred his way.

"What…" she demanded, when they were face to face, "are those filthy creatures doing on *my* boat?" She didn't give him a chance to answer. "In fact, I don't *care* what they're doing," she added through gritted teeth. "Get rid of them at once. Throw them overboard!"

3

The Fairy Godtingy

Skipper Ed could feel his jaw jutting.

"If you don't want them," he demanded, "why did you bring them?"

Alice was astonished. "*Bring* them?" She looked at her unfortunate assistant. "Is this another of your mistakes, Deidre, poppet?"

"No, Miss Barton—"

"What are they going on about?" murmured Oxo to Wills.

"I can't hear properly. They're too far away. But, um, I think she wants to throw us in the sea," replied Wills awkwardly.

"Ohmygrassohmygrass!" squeaked Jaycey. "Can I swim?"

"Man," said Links to Wills, "I thought you said the Alice Barton dude was on our side?"

"Now, Links, dear," said Sal. "Wills *is* only a lamb,

remember, and lambs do make mistakes. It's part of growing up."

"And now his growin' up's finished. We's gonna drown. That's almost the same as dyin'.'"

"I'm sorry, guys," Wills said quietly. "Maybe she's a wicked witch, not a fairy godmother."

Alice raised her voice a little. "Well, Ted? What are you waiting for? I told you to ditch them."

"Can't, I'm afraid," replied Ed. His jaw was jutting out even farther.

"Can't?"

"It's against regulations."

"What regulations?"

"The Non-Disposal of Fleeced Animals in the Sea regulations." Ed had just made this up. He glared at Alice, defying her to argue.

Bur she didn't. She leaned closer until her nose was almost touching his. "Then *slaughter* them," she hissed quietly. "You can have lamb chops for supper every day for a month."

When Alice had gone, quietly closing her cabin door behind her, Ed and Deidre stood looking at each other.

"You any good at butchering?" asked Ed.

Deidre shuddered. "Oh, I couldn't."

"Me neither." Ed sighed and called to a deckhand. "Make room for them in number two hold," he ordered. "Out of sight, out of mind."

A few minutes later, the sheep were following the deckhand down some stairs to a small but airy hold on the other side of the boat.

Sal looked around the hold approvingly. "How very pleasant," she said. "You see, she's already assisting us."

"Who is?" asked Oxo, scoffing some cauliflower the deckhand had thrown in.

"The, um, you know…"

"Fairy godtingy," supplied Links helpfully.

"Exactly. Our fairy godtingy. Just as Wills predicted she would."

Wills tried to protest. He was very confused. "But she told the Ed man to ditch us. That means—"

"No, no, no, dear." Sal beamed triumphantly. "I'm sure she didn't say ditch. I expect she said *dip*."

Wills blinked. The other warriors stared.

"Of course," conceded Sal. "Being dipped is not pleasant. None of us likes being pushed into a tank of stinky water, but it's for our own good. That's why Ida does it every spring: to stop us getting scab and other nasty diseases."

Wills was even more confused but he didn't have the chance to say more because Sal had closed her eyes and was beginning to sway slightly.

"Hello, she's off again," muttered Oxo.

"The sheeply warriors brave and true…" cried Sal,
"Will need some help to find that Ewe.
A human, strange in word and deed,
Will be their star and take the lead.
Through foaming waters, Outback dire,
Through thirst and famine, mud and mire,
Her actions may seem *odd*, it's true…"

Sal opened one eye meaningfully.

"But if they want to save the Ewe,
They must stay by the human's side,
They must stay close, for she's their guide…"

Sal opened both eyes and smiled at Wills. "Does that help?"

"Er, yes…I think so."

Jaycey added excitedly, "If we stay close, she might give me some hoof varnish."

"What is written is written," announced Sal.

And nobody could really argue with that.

4
Barton's Billabong

It was evening back at Murkton-on-Sea, and Rose was getting more and more worried. She'd looked everywhere for the sheep. She was beginning to feel guilty too. What if they'd fallen into the harbor and drowned? So when her sister Ida phoned, she didn't know what to say. Fortunately, Ida did most of the talking.

"Lovely morning here at Barton's Billabong," she said. "And guess what, we've got another joey."

"Another what?" asked Rose, vaguely.

"Joey," repeated Ida. "You know, baby kangaroo. It's an orphan. Like Wills. We've popped it into a pillowcase so it thinks it's still in its mother's pouch."

"Lovely," said Rose.

"How is Wills?" asked Ida. "And all our super sheep?"

"Super," said Rose. "Just super."

"And when are we going to Skype?"

"Pardon?"

"Skype, dear. You know. We set up your computer for you before we left—with the little webcam and everything—so you can see our joeys and possums and we can say hello to our sheep."

"Oh, right," said Rose.

"Have you had a technical glitch?" asked Ida.

"Sort of. Yes."

"Shall I put Tod on, to talk you through it?"

"No. Not just now," said Rose quickly. "I've got a cake in the oven. Must go. Byee." And she quickly pressed the button to end the call.

• • •

Down Under at Barton's Billabong, Ida frowned at Tod. "Rose sounded a bit funny," she said.

"Probably just the connection, Gran," said Tod. "She's a long way away."

"So are our sheep," said Ida. "I do hope they're all right."

"Why wouldn't they be?" asked Frank as he came in for breakfast.

Ida's brother Frank was almost as old as she was. And almost as much fun. He'd been in Australia for most of his life and his face was as rutted as the

28

reddish-brown dirt tracks around the little house he lived in here at Barton's Billabong. He'd always kept in touch with his sisters, Rose and Ida, and Ida's grandson, Tod—who was really her great-grandson and who lived with Ida because he too was an orphan. They all wrote letters and emailed and talked on the phone, so when Frank had offered to pay for Ida and Tod to visit him, they'd been delighted to accept.

"And how's sister Rose?" he asked. "Didn't she Skype so you could say g'day to your fancy flock?"

"No," said Tod. "She's got a glitch."

"As long as it's not catching," said Frank. "We've got a busy day ahead. You're not just on vacation, y'know."

Frank had worked at Barton's Billabong for more than fifty years and he loved the place. It was an animal sanctuary, way out in the bush: the lovely, lonely, wild part of Australia. Not so lonely that it didn't have roads, though, which meant that the sanctuary always had a dozen or so baby kangaroos, joeys, in its nursery.

Kangaroos never learned to look both ways when crossing roads and lots were knocked down each year. Often the mother would be killed in the accident, but her baby, cushioned in her pouch, would survive. These babies were brought to Barton's Billabong, where each one would be given a pillowcase of its own, hung from a bar, so they could hop in and out of this pretend pouch whenever they liked. The littlest ones stayed inside for a long time, only their noses and front paws peeping out.

The sanctuary had been set up long ago by two kindly half-brothers, Motte and Bailey Barton, and Frank had been as fond of them as of his work. Had been, because Motte had died a few months ago and Bailey had passed away just a week later. This had made Frank very sad and made him think of his own family, far away in Britain, and want to see them again.

"The old boys had a good run," Frank sighed as he led Tod and Ida on their first proper tour of the sanctuary. "Left this world a better place than they found it."

"So what will happen to the sanctuary?" asked Tod.

"And you, Frank?" asked Ida anxiously. "I hope you won't lose your home?"

Frank grinned. "I shouldn't think so. Motte and Bailey didn't have any children of their own, but they thought they had a great-great niece somewhere. So they left the sanctuary and the land and everything to her."

"I don't understand," said Tod. "How can you only *think* you have a niece somewhere?"

Frank ruffled Tod's hair. "You have to remember, mate, we didn't have email and social networking and all that stuff when we were young. The Bartons were working their socks off setting up this place and they lost touch with their family years ago."

"So how will anybody find this niece?" asked Ida, still concerned for Frank's future.

"She *has* been found." said Frank. "Through a lawyer. A guy in Brisbane. Goes by the wonderful name of Joseph Creeply. He put ads in the papers and on the net and...everywhere. And the lady replied. She's got the birth certificate and everything."

"So where is she?" said Tod and Ida together.

Frank grinned. "Motte and Bailey were both very proud to be Down Underers. Motte was born in New Zealand and Bailey in Australia, and they had a bit of a sense of humor. So their will says this niece has got to prove herself to be a good Down Underer too. They set her a few little tasks she has to do before she can inherit. And she's got to do them before the thirtieth of November."

"Hmm," said Ida, not at all sure about this strange condition the old men had put on their will. "And what's her name?"

"Alice," said Frank. "Alice Barton."

"And what's she like?" asked Ida.

Frank shrugged. "No idea. But if she's related to Motte and Bailey, she's bound to be as good as gold."

5
Down Under

Through the many days and nights that followed, *Destiny* forged rapidly southward across the oceans, rarely within sight of land and never stopping. Fuel and food were piped and heaved aboard from supply boats.

The sheep stayed hidden in their little hold, fed and cleaned by the deckhand, who let them out occasionally when Alice wasn't on deck. And every evening, Wills told his fellow warriors all the stories he could remember from Tod's book about knights in armor and castles.

Meanwhile, Alice spent every day sweating away in her gym. The solicitor, Mr. Creeply, had refused to say what sort of challenges the deceased uncles, Motte and Bailey, had set, but she was worried they could be sporty-type things. And she hadn't done so much as run for a bus since she left school.

Then, one beautiful sunny day when the warriors were stretching their legs on deck and Alice was trying to pump iron, Wills heard a shout from one of the crew.

"Down Under ahoy!" he repeated excitedly for the others. "That means we're there!"

They crowded against the boat's rail, peering ahead at the shoreline that was slowly getting nearer. Soon, *Destiny* was passing close to the hundreds of yachts moored in the vast Auckland harbor and the warriors heard the same sound that had first called them, back in Murkton-on-Sea.

"Ohmygrass…" said Jaycey. "It's tacky Tuftella."

"Yeah, still sobbing and sighing and tap, tap, tapping," agreed Links.

Wills glanced uneasily at the yachts but put the thought that it might be them making the sound firmly out of his mind. It was far too late for doubt. They were almost in New Zealand. Part of Down Under. Somewhere out there, Tuftella was waiting to be rescued.

Ed and Deidre were standing on the deck, not far from the little bunch of sheep.

"New Zealand has strict rules about bringing animals into the country, you know," said Ed. "It could mean a long delay. Who's going to tell her about the sheep? You or me?"

Alice suddenly appeared in her pink-and-white designer gym-wear.

"Ted, poppet," she inquired. "Why aren't we going full steam...ahead?" Her smile froze on her lips. She'd seen the sheep.

"What are *they* doing here?"

"Um...a bit of a misunderstanding," said Ed. "And we, uh, won't be allowed to berth until we've got permission." He didn't drop his eyes from her angry face, though. "It'll only take a few days."

"A few *days*?" Alice glared at him. "I do not *have* a few days." She clenched her fists and her face began to flush. "Get me ashore. *Now*."

Ed folded his arms and shook his head. "I can't go any closer," he said. "Not with sheep on-board."

The simmering volcano that was Alice erupted. Her face now a scarlet ball, she ran at the unsuspecting flock.

"Deidre!" she yelled. "Chuck them off!"

"Miss Barton?"

"The sheep, you dishcloth. Throw them overboard!"

The warriors stared as their fairy godtingy hurled

herself at them, grabbed Wills by his front legs, and threw him into the sea.

6
Lamb Overboard

L amb overboard!" yelled Ed. "Stop engines!"

But his voice was drowned out by the sound of Deidre screaming and the other sheep bleating.

"Ohmygrassohmygrass..." squealed Jaycey, as Alice caught hold of her hind legs. "Ohmylegsohmy..." The rest was lost in the splash as she hit the water.

Alice turned to Oxo next, but he was already charging after Wills and Jaycey, determined to rescue them. He skidded under the rail and plummeted into the waves.

"Ram overboard!" shouted Ed. "Half astern both!"

"Aye, aye, skip," came a call from the bridge.

Meanwhile, the question Jaycey had asked some days ago was answered. She *could* swim. She didn't enjoy it, but somehow she instinctively paddled with her front legs and her head stayed above water.

On deck, Alice was pushing Sal's rear end. "Move!" she grunted. "We haven't got time to mess about!"

Sal stood planted firmly on the deck, thinking. The words she wanted finally came back. "Her actions may seem odd, it's true," she bleated loudly. "Verse…" She couldn't remember which verse but it didn't matter. She suddenly leapt forward, over the rail and into the sea. Alice fell flat on her face. Links couldn't help treading on her as he jumped into the water after Sal.

"Full astern both!" roared Ed. "We're going to run them down!"

"No!" shouted Alice, picking herself up. "Full *ahead* both!"

But *Destiny* was now moving backward, fast. Unfortunately, there was a large fishing boat close behind. Too close. There was a crunch of metal on metal and a violent jolt.

"Now look what you've done!" Alice cried at Ed. "Just capture a yacht or something and get me ashore!"

Deidre was weeping noisily as she peered over *Destiny*'s side. All she could see was foaming white water and deck furniture that had bounced over the guard rail into the sea. "They're gone," she sobbed. "Drowned. Those poor sheep have drowned…"

"Well," said Alice, "that's one consolation."

But the warriors hadn't drowned. An onshore wind was sweeping them rapidly toward land. They coughed and choked and paddled desperately, their white heads more often under the water than above it. They were completely hidden amid the white topped waves.

Wills saw a small upturned plastic table swirling toward him. He turned his body to face the way the table was moving and waited until it was right up close to him. Then he threw his front hooves on to it and dragged his hindquarters aboard. The upturned table rocked violently from side to side but Wills managed to stay upright.

"Find yourselves something to float on!" he yelled at the others.

More upturned tables from *Destiny*'s sun deck were being swept in, along with dozens of large empty boxes lost from the fishing boat in the collision. One by one, the other Warrior Sheep copied Wills and managed to haul themselves out of the water. Sal lay sprawled on her tummy across her table. Jaycey crouched as low as she could inside her smelly fish box. Oxo stood squarely on top of a box marked *Bait*, and Links crouched athletically on another upturned table.

The choppy waves became a swelling line of surf, rolling in toward the beach near the harbor, sweeping the warriors with it.

"Surf's up, man!" yelled Links. "These waves is crankin'!"

His wave rose. "Cowabunga!" he cried in triumph. His wave crashed. Links lost his balance and was submerged before being tumbled head over tail up the beach. He staggered to his feet, spluttering. "Duh… think that's what you call a wipeout. Still, we's pretty cool, eh, guys? Like woolly fish, right?"

Oxo didn't give an opinion. He was using his great head to push Sal clear of the water.

Wills and Jaycey had reached the beach too.

Links was beaming. "High hooves for the surfing dudes?"

The others stopped coughing and shaking water from their fleeces and turned to Links. They each raised a front hoof and clacked them all together.

"High hooves!" they shouted. "Warrior Sheep Down Under!"

"But only just," said Wills. "We could have been drowned. Or crushed. We were lucky."

"Luck had nothing do with it, dear," Sal said happily. "It was our fairy godtingy who saved us."

The others stopped grinning and stared at her.

"Surely it's obvious," she continued. "She *knew* the boat was going to crash and pushed us over the side to save our lives."

7
Shelly and Trevor

It took some time before Alice could get ashore. For a start, the skipper of the fishing boat was a very angry man, who exchanged rather rude words with her. And then her own skipper, Captain Ted, told her that *Destiny*'s propellers were badly damaged and the boat wouldn't move no matter how much she told it to. Finally, Alice smiled sweetly at the owner of a nearby dinghy, and he took her and her luggage and Deidre to the quayside.

When they finally landed, Alice fixed her makeup, while Deidre made some phone calls for her. Then they perched on a bench overlooking the harbor. Deidre sniffed back more tears as she gazed at the oily water and imagined the poor sheep drowned beneath it. Alice glanced briefly at the tugs chugging out to pull *Destiny* in to the repair dock.

"Well, what did the insurance company say?" she asked.

"I'm afraid they're unlikely to pay for the damage," replied Deidre.

"Whyever not?"

"Something about it being an 'Act of Sheep.'"

Alice ground her teeth but let the matter drop. "Well, get the laptop out, poppet," she said briskly. "Let's get started on claiming my inheritance. What do I have to do first?"

Deidre opened Alice's mailbox. There was an email from Joseph Creeply, Attorney at Law. She read aloud. "For your first challenge, you must go to Rotapangi, where you will"—Deidre caught her breath—"do a *bungee* jump!" She stared wide-eyed at Alice, then read the last line. "I will require photographic proof that you have completed this and every challenge. Good luck."

"Good luck!" squeaked Alice. "You need more than *luck* to bungee jump."

"Too right," said a voice above their heads. "You need a good strong piece of elastic."

Alice looked up slowly at the dusty boots, the sturdy, sun-tanned legs, the slightly ragged shorts, the faded bush shirt, and the weathered, cheerful face of the young woman looking down at them. Their owner smiled broadly.

"G'day. I'm Shelly. I guess you're Alice. You hired me." She held out her hand. "Saw you arrive just now." Her grin broadened. "Top show."

Alice gave the newcomer a smile that wasn't a smile and didn't shake her hand. "To my employees," she explained precisely, "I'm Miss Barton."

"Sure, Alice," said Shelly. "Whatever."

Alice turned back to Deidre. "Is this really the best you could find, poppet, mm?"

"Uh, yes, Miss Barton. I mean…she's qualified in all sorts of sports and stuff and knows first aid and can cook and drive and…"

"And I know New Zealand and Oz like the back of my bush hat," finished Shelly. "I've been leading adventure tour groups for years. Got my own transport too, of course."

Alice looked Shelly up and down again. She was going to have to make the best of a bad job. She braced herself and stood up. "Right," she said. "Take me to Rotapangi. Bring the stuff with you, Deidre."

Shelly looked from Alice to Deidre, then at the

mountain of luggage. She picked up the two heaviest suitcases as if they were filled with feathers and strode off. "That's what I like to see," she said. "Traveling light."

Deidre hurried behind with the laptop and remaining bags.

• • •

The warriors had felt the need for a reviving snack after their first ever try at surfing. They wandered back toward the harbor, found a patch of grass in a quiet corner near a parking lot, and got their noses down.

"Nice grass…" mumbled Oxo, tearing at it greedily. "Salty, like it was at Murkton-on-Sea."

"The sobbing and sighing and tap, tap, tapping's the same too, actually," pointed out Jaycey. She still wasn't sure she wanted to meet the fairest ewe of all, but with their stomachs full and the sunshine drying their fleeces, the warriors all felt excited again.

Links looked up and began to nod:

"Miss Tuftella, you ain't got nothin' to fear,
Well, I s'pose you have but we's gettin' near.
We's the surfin' sheep with a one track mind,
That's tellin' us just what we gotta find.

We's Down Under now and there's somethin' new,
So listen up, girl, and hear me true.
The fairy godtingy's showin' the way,
So, Tuftella, tune in to what we gotta say:
Between us all, we's got the power,
An' we's comin' to get you from your dark ol'
    tower."

The other warriors joined in.

"Yes, we's comin' to get you from you dark ol'
    tower!"

Oxo suddenly broke off in mid-chorus and stared. "Hey, guys—isn't that her over there? Our fairy godtingy!"

The sheep looked up and saw Alice Barton hurrying across the parking lot, trying to keep up with a woman who was carrying a large suitcase in each hand. The Deidre girl was running along behind them, carrying more bags, which she kept dropping, then stopping to pick up. The woman with the big suitcases dumped them next to a battered four-wheel-drive truck on the far side of the parking lot.

• • •

"Say hello to Trevor," said Shelly. "He's your trusty conveyance for the next few days. Or weeks. Or however long it takes you to do what you have to do in New Zealand."

"I presume you *are* joking?" said Alice, staring in disbelief at the dust-coated vehicle.

"Don't be rude about Trevor," said Shelly. "We've been through a lot together." She opened the passenger door. "Get in, find a seat. You've got plenty of choice. We usually carry six passengers."

Alice turned on Deidre. "Can't you do anything right? Why didn't you check what sort of vehicle she had?"

"But they're all the same," said Deidre. "All the adventure tour companies have trucks like this."

"I don't do *trucks*, poppet!" said Alice. "I do cars. Sleek, fast, expensive cars."

"Not in the Outback you don't," said Shelly. "Or most of New Zealand. Certainly not Rotapangi." She went round to the back of the truck. It was parked very close to a low wall. She jumped up onto the wall and, from there, onto the truck's roof. It had a guardrail all around it and straps to tie down the rucksacks that it usually carried. "Hand up your bags and I'll tie them on top," she called.

Alice sat down firmly on her largest suitcase. "What *do* you think I am?" she demanded. "A backpacker? I have proper clothes. Expensive clothes. I have beauty products. I have office equipment. They are *not* going up there."

Shelly shrugged. "Suit yourself. But you'll be cramped inside."

Alice stood up and nodded toward the open door of the truck. "Deidre."

"Yes, Miss Barton." Deidre heaved the heaviest case into the truck and dumped it on the nearest seat. Alice stood glaring up at Shelly until all the bags were in. Then she shoved Deidre in after them.

"You can sit at the back," she said to her. "It's bound to be the bumpiest place, so please don't be sick." She climbed in after Deidre and slammed the door.

• • •

At the edge of the parking lot, the sheep were suddenly thrown into a panic.

"Ohmgrassohymyfairygodtingy…" wailed Jaycey. "She's going. And taking all her lotions and potions with her!"

"Follow, follow!" called Sal. "She is our guide. We must stay by her side!"

With Sal in the lead, the five sheep galloped across the parking lot.

Shelly didn't see them coming because she'd turned her back to jump down from the roof again. She squeezed into the driver's seat. "OK, let's rock to Rotapangi," she said and turned the key.

"Quickly, quickly...!" bleated Sal, her fat bottom swaying from side to side as she ran.

"Onto the wall!" shouted Wills. He leapt up and ran along it, beside the slowly moving truck. The others, even Sal, managed to leap up after him. Except Oxo, who dived straight over the top and had to jump back from the other side.

"Oops," he grunted. "Overdid it a bit."

His hooves landed on the wall just as Wills hopped onto the roof of the truck.

"Now!" Wills called. "Jump. All of you!"

Thumpety, thumpety, thumpety, thump!

The truck swayed as the four remaining warriors obeyed Wills's command and jumped from the wall onto the moving roof.

• • •

"What a *wonderful* vehicle," sighed Alice from inside the truck. "Even the roof makes a racket."

Shelly merely assumed the noise was the expensive suitcases falling about behind her. Deidre was already feeling too sick to notice anything.

• • •

On the roof, the sheep were getting their breath back.

"She could have given us time to finish lunch," complained Oxo.

"Sit down and wedge yourselves against the rails," advised Wills.

"Ohmygrassohmyfleeceohmyeverything..." cried Jaycey as Shelly put her foot on the accelerator and the truck sped toward the highway. The pretty Jacob sat down quickly before she toppled overboard. The warriors on the roof pressed safely together, and before long they were enjoying the wind in their fleeces.

• • •

Inside, Alice settled into her seat. "Deidre. Find me some gentle music," she called, without turning round. "I need de-stressing. It's been a traumatic day." She heaved a sigh. "Still, at least I've got rid of those mangy sheep."

8
Maiden Tower

Tod and Ida had soon got into the swing of things at Barton's Billabong. Rose still hadn't sorted out her Skyping, so they still hadn't seen their sheep back in Murkton, but that was the only drawback to being Down Under. And Frank was cheerful again.

"D'you guys like cricket?" he asked one morning.

He knew very well that Tod and Ida both loved cricket. All sports, in fact.

Tod grinned. "Gran's a wicked bowler."

"You might like these, then," said Frank, and he pushed an envelope across the table.

Ida looked at him suspiciously. "Is this one of your jokes?" she inquired. "I'm not opening it if it's full of spiders."

Frank took back the envelope. "Fair enough. I'll see if the joeys want to go."

"Go where?" asked Tod eagerly.

"Only Brisbane." Frank shrugged. "Only England against Australia. Only the first test match of the series."

"What?" Tod leapt in the air. "A test match, Gran! Howzat!"

Ida grabbed the envelope and batted Frank round the ear with it. "Well," she said, laughing, "since we're here in Oz, I suppose we might as well."

"But what about you, Uncle Frank?" asked Tod.

"Oh, I'll watch it on the TV."

Ida suddenly felt a bit bad about leaving Frank. "But surely Nat could look after the place for a couple of days?"

Nat was Frank's assistant.

"He could," said Frank. "But he's new and it wouldn't be fair to leave him on his own. Anyway, I haven't left this place for years. I don't think I want to start again now." He tossed a baby's feeding bottle to Tod. "Come on, mate. Dinner duty."

It was roasting hot outside the house. Frank, Ida, and Tod walked slowly across the yard to the nursery, the shady corner where the line of pillowcases hung. They each took a little joey in their arms and sat down under the shade of a gum tree. The joeys whimpered and wriggled until they had their mouths clamped firmly around the teats on the bottles, then they settled down to slurp greedily.

Nat walked past, pushing a wheelbarrow loaded with dirty straw from one of the pens he was cleaning.

"G'day, Nat," said Frank. "How y'doing? Need any help with that?"

Nat shook his head. "No worries," he said. He was a big, strong man in his mid-twenties, with a suntanned face and cropped dark hair. He wore shorts and a bush shirt, like almost everybody else. He nodded at Ida and Tod as he strode past.

"He seems a nice young man," said Ida.

"Yeah. He's good," agreed Frank. "Doesn't have much to say for himself but that suits me. Most folks talk too much. And I really need his help now that..." He swallowed hard. "Well, now that Motte and Bailey aren't around to do their bit."

"Uncle Frank," said Tod. "Why do you call them Motte and Bailey? What were their real names?"

"Those *were* their real names," laughed Frank. "Their father was English and nuts about history. Especially medieval history. So he called his first son Motte, like the hill that castles used to be built on. Then he called his second son Bailey, like the big wall and courtyard they used to build around castles."

Tod giggled. "So if he'd had a third son, he could have called him Keep. Or Drawbridge."

Frank took the teat from the joey's mouth for a minute to give it a rest from sucking. "Probably would have done," he said. "Motte and Bailey were pretty keen on history too. Not to say nutty like their dad. They built the tower. Even dug the moat around it and filled it with water from the creek."

"I was wondering about the tower," said Ida, taking the empty bottle from her joey's mouth and popping the little creature gently back in its pillowcase. "What's it used for," she asked.

The circular stone tower stood on an island in the middle of its water-filled moat, which was like a small lake. The tower was five floors high, with just one tiny window on each floor. A huge brass padlock hung from the heavy front door. And the only way to get to it was across a narrow bridge. The floor of the bridge was made of ropes, woven together, and there was just one rope on either side to hold on to.

"What's it used for?" repeated Frank. "Just the

office. Motte and Bailey used to do all their paperwork and stuff in there. It's always cool, see. A good place to store things away from the damp and the ants. Never likely to go up in flames either, and that's important with all these gum trees around."

"Have you ever been inside?" asked Ida.

"Oh, yeah," said Frank. "I used to help out a bit with the money side of things. But not since they died."

"Why not?"

Frank shrugged. "The solicitor, Mr. Creeply, came over right away and locked it up. Said nobody was to go in until he'd had a chance to go through all the papers and accounts and bank books and stuff."

"But that was months ago," said Tod.

Frank shrugged. "Solicitors tend not to rush things."

"Well, I hope he gets on with it soon," said Ida. "The place looks like it could do with a good clean. You can hardly see through the windows."

"You can tell Mr. Creeply that when you meet him," said Frank with a grin. "He's supposed to be paying us a visit any day now."

Nat trundled past again with a barrow load of fresh straw.

"Looking forward to it, aren't we, Nat?" called Frank.

"Not a lot," grunted Nat. "Who wants a pen-pusher getting in the way?"

"It's a bit over the top for an office," said Tod. "It looks really strong."

"Oh, it is," said Frank. "You'd need a battering ram to get through the door. Building it properly was a sort of hobby with the old boys."

"Does it have a name?" Tod asked suddenly.

"Course it does," said Frank. "It's called Maiden Tower."

9
Not Maiden Tower

The Rotapangi Road House was a rambling, homely backpackers' hostel at the end of a winding track. Shelly parked Trevor next to a row of other trucks and jumped down from behind the wheel. The place was teeming with young men and women in shorts and T-shirts. And they were all laughing. The drivers of the other trucks were laughing too.

"Nice one, Shel," called one of the drivers. "You started doing sheep shearing holidays?"

Shelly frowned, then looked up.

"Holy-moly…" she gasped. Then she laughed with everyone else.

• • •

On Trevor's roof, the Warrior Sheep were standing up stiffly and peering at the ground. The journey had been fun in a jaw-jarring way, but none of them were sure what to expect next.

"How we gonna get down there?" asked Links.

"Never fear," said Sal. "Our fairy godtingy will show us what to do."

• • •

Alice emerged from the truck. "What's so funny?" she asked irritably. Then she too saw the sheep. She took a deep breath and shouted.

"Deidre? Deidre!"

Deidre was climbing out over the bags and suit-cases. She stumbled to the ground, still feeling sick.

"Is this *your* doing?"

"No, Miss Barton, of course not," breathed Deidre, wide-eyed and wobbling. "But isn't it wonderful they didn't drown."

Alice made no reply. She turned to Shelly, seething quietly. "*Your* problem, not mine. Just dispose of them. Terminally would be good."

Shelly wasn't short of different advice from the other drivers.

"You could drive round in circles and make 'em dizzy so they fall off..."

"Or cut a hole in Trevor's roof so they drop through..."

"Or hire a helicopter and—"

"Bring us some sleeping bags," called Shelly to the watching backpackers. "And sweaters. Anything soft except your socks. We're not trying to gas the poor guys. Give us those," she added to Deidre, who was struggling to haul suitcases out of the truck.

Shelly grabbed two of the nicest cases and dumped them on the ground. "They'll make a good solid base," she said, nudging them into position with her boot and daring Alice to argue.

A dozen willing hands were now dragging and stacking the rest of the luggage, then draping and padding it with grubby sleeping bags.

• • •

Gazing down at the activity around the ever-rising pile, Wills said, "I think they want us to jump off."

"There," said Sal, beaming, "Didn't I tell you she would find a way?" And without warning, she leapt from the roof.

The backpackers scattered as Sal whumped down on to their landing pad. They stayed well back as Oxo then Links quickly followed. Jaycey teetered on the edge for a moment.

"Ohmygrass...What if I chip something?"

"Just go for it," said Wills. So Jaycey did and landed safely. She hopped out of the way before Wills could jump on top of her. Wills, being only a lamb, sprang from the roof and landed lightly on the heap, where he enjoyed bouncing up and down for longer than he needed to.

"That's enough, dear," said Sal. "You're getting too old to show off like that."

Alice was peering around angrily. "Where's my hotel?" she demanded.

Shelly nodded at the Rotapangi Road House. "You're looking at it. There's nothing else around here. It's that or sleep in Trevor."

Alice's mouth pursed into a tiny, cross crinkle. Then she smiled. "Very well, but be aware, Shelly, I shall remember all these little moments. Go and book my bungee jump while I check in. And Deidre…"

"Yes, Miss Barton, I know. Bring the bags."

Alice stalked away. She was at the front door of the hostel before she realized that the little flock of sheep were close at her heels.

"You can't bring your pets inside, sweetheart," said the man at the reception desk.

"They are *not* my pets," Alice said icily. "And I am *not* your sweetheart."

The receptionist shrugged and shut the door. "The woollies can stay round the back in the yard, if you like. You're in dorm number two. It's on the first floor."

Alice gulped. "Dorm?"

"Dorm," repeated the receptionist. "As in dormitory?"

"As in sharing my sleeping place with strangers?"

"Ah, they won't be strangers for long. Not once they've broken wind and clipped their toenails on your bunk and talked all night." He slapped a key into her hand. "Enjoy!"

• • •

The sheep stood with their noses against the hostel front door.

"Has the fairy godtingy gone?" asked Jaycey.

"Only for a moment, I'm sure," said Sal. "We must stay here and wait for her."

Oxo's tum rumbled loudly. "Waiting on an empty stomach's bad for you," he announced firmly. "I smell proper pasture." And he trotted off, leading the way behind the parked trucks to the nearby riverbank.

The Rotapangi River was wide and very fast. The

water tumbled and raced along, bubbling in pools, swirling around hidden rocks, and crashing over falls. The grass on the bank was trodden down by the hundreds of human boots that walked on it every day, but it was still the nearest thing to a decent field the sheep had seen in a long time.

Wills chomped for a while, then straightened up, gazing along the river. He'd noticed something a little farther along the bank: a tall, thin metal structure. Was it...could it be...a tower? The Maiden Tower that the fairy godtingy had talked to someone on the phone about, back on *Destiny*? It didn't *look* like the ancient tower that Wills had seen in Tod's book, but maybe there were different sorts. And he *could* see what looked like a little room at the top. The maiden in distress in Tod's book, he remembered, had been locked in a little room at the top of her tower. Then again, the tower he was staring at had a metal platform outside the room and a rope dangling from the platform, directly above the river. Wills was perplexed. He put his head down and resumed grazing.

• • •

There were just two bunks left in dorm number two. The rest were piled with other people's rucksacks.

"I'll have the top one," said Alice to Deidre. "You can have the bottom. You don't mind sharing with the luggage, do you, poppet?" She climbed up to the top bunk. "I've got a few calls to make while you fetch it. Run along."

It took Deidre three trips to lug all the bags up to the dorm. As she puffed in with the last load, Shelly bounded in past her.

"Sorted," she said, waving a fistful of papers. "I've booked your bungee jump. You've got five minutes."

"Five minutes?" said Alice, going pale.

"Last slot of the day. After that, they've got a film crew booked in."

"Ooh," gasped Deidre, dumping the bags. "Anyone famous?"

"No, just some kind of animal show called *Almost Human*." Shelly turned and frowned. "You good to go in that?" she asked, nodding at Alice who today was wearing white trousers and a sequined shirt.

"Some of us don't do scruff, poppet." Alice smiled sweetly.

"Your choice," said Shelly and she bounded off again, back down the stairs. "Come on, let's get the lady weighed in."

Alice hesitated, then followed. Pausing in the doorway, she turned to Deidre. "Stay here and guard the bags."

"Yes, Miss Barton. Good luck, Miss Barton. Remember to smile for the photo." Then, in a rare moment of defiance, Deidre added under her breath, "Boing... boing...boing..." Fortunately, her employer didn't hear.

"Why do I have to be weighed?" Alice demanded when she caught up with Shelly outside. She was a little sensitive on the subject.

"So you don't smash headfirst into the river," said Shelly. "They need to know how far you'll stretch the bungee elastic. The heavier you are, the more it'll stretch. So every one gets weighed and then the guys can adjust the length of the bungee rope accordingly. Yes? Good. In there."

They were on the riverbank now and Shelly indicated a small hut.

The man in the hut noted Alice's weight as she stepped off the scales.

"OK," he said. "Sign here, please."

"Why?"

"To say that if anything goes wrong it's not our fault." He grinned. "Only joking. It just says you're fit enough and healthy enough and mad enough to jump into space."

Alice's hand began to tremble as she signed the form.

Shelly was waiting outside the hut. "All set?" she asked brightly when Alice emerged.

Alice didn't answer. The tower reared above the river. An open-work metal structure like a ladder to the sky. The cabin at the top and the platform outside it, a tiny dot in the distance. Staring up, Alice gulped. And that's when the sheep saw her.

10
Almost Human

M ook!" mumbled Wills excitedly through a mouthful of grass. "Mour mairy mobmimmy!" He spat out the grass. "Over there. By the tower!"

"*Tower?*" A collective grassy gasp swept through the little flock. They all remembered the stories of warriors and maidens in distress that Wills had told them while they were on the boat. They stared at their fairy god-tingy walking toward the tower. Then they set off in pursuit at a gallop.

"She never lets us finish eating..." grumbled Oxo, racing to overtake Sal and everyone else. He saw it as his duty to be in front whenever any charging about had to be done.

• • •

At the base of the tower, the door to the small cage-like elevator stood open. Its cheerful attendant was checking Alice's paperwork.

"They'll gear you up nice and safely at the top," she said. "Our bungee's the strongest bit of stretchy rope in the Universe."

Alice swallowed hard but said nothing .

"It's easy," continued the girl. "You just hold your arms out on either side of your body and lean forward like you're a swallow flying. That's all there is to it. You'll tip over headfirst and the elastic'll stop you just above the water."

Alice's face was now the color of gray mud.

Shelly gave her a kindly pat on the shoulder. "You'll be fine. And don't forget to—"

"Yes," snapped Alice. "I know. Smile for the photo."

The next moment, Shelly was knocked off her feet by a hurtling wedge of wool and hooves. Alice was slammed against the back of the elevator cage with a stack of smelly, panting sheep pressed against her.

"What *is* it with you ragbags?" Alice gasped. "What do you *want*!?"

Wills would have thought this a strange question from a fairy godtingy, but he was squashed beneath Oxo's bottom and didn't hear it.

"Oh, I get it," said the elevator girl. "You're *Almost*

Human. Great program." She closed the door on the elevator's bulging load and sent it on its way.

As the cage creaked upward, Jaycey asked, "Is this Maiden Tower, then?"

"Almost certainly, dear," said Sal. "Our fairy god-tingy is showing us the way."

"So why can't we hear tacky Tuftella," said Jaycey, "if she's up here?"

"Good question," said Links, glancing anxiously at the ground, now far below. "There is a total absence of moanin', right?"

"*And* we haven't fought off any snapping monsters yet," pointed out Oxo, sounding rather disappointed.

The elevator cage jolted to a halt and the door opened. The sheep tumbled out into a little cabin. Alice followed. Her knees were turning to rubber. Through the opening opposite she could see a narrow ledge. Then space. Beside the ledge was a spindle, like a huge cotton reel bolted to the platform. And round the spindle was wound the elastic rope that would shortly be fixed to her ankles. Before she jumped.

The sheep were nosing around the tiny cabin, searching for the maiden in distress. The jumpmaster and her assistant were confused and agitated.

"So are you Alice Barton or *Almost Human*?" demanded the jumpmaster.

And in that split second, Alice saw a way to avoid the dreaded leap.

"I'm *Almost Human*, of course," she replied, like the top TV person she wasn't.

The jumpmaster turned away for a moment. "Keep those sheep away from the edge!" she shouted at her assistant.

"Yes, do," said Alice. "We actually only need one. That one." She pointed at Sal.

Sal nodded modestly at her fellow warriors. "Oh—I seem to have been chosen for something," she said.

Alice smiled breezily at the jumpmaster. "So, let's do it up or whatever the technical term is," she ordered.

The jumpmaster frowned. "What, for a jump? We can't make an animal *jump*!"

"Of course not, you silly girl," trilled Alice. "I just want it to *look* as if it's going to jump. *Almost Human*? Yes? Our clever film guys will do the rest."

The jumpmaster sighed and shrugged dubiously,

but nodded at her assistant. "OK, but keep the rest of them well back."

Apart from Oxo, who was testing the bungee rope on its spindle for chewability, the rest of the warriors watched with interest as Sal's hind ankles were wrapped in nylon padding, then strapped tightly together. The assistant shooed Oxo away from the bungee rope and attached it through a plastic cone to the strapping around Sal's ankles.

Alice forced herself to walk out onto the ledge. She laughed gaily as she pressed her designer sunglasses onto Sal's face. Alice would never have admitted she was sheep-shaped, but this one might just pass for her at a hundred miles an hour. And she was desperate enough to try anything. She just had to make her shove look like an accident.

"Nice sheep..." she said, crouching close to Sal. She wasn't great with animals. "Nice sheepikins..."

• • •

But Sal wasn't listening. She was hobbling straight past the fairy godtingy, trailing the bungee rope behind her. Somewhere, beyond the edge of the platform, she could hear a sound she was sure she understood. A sobbing and sighing.

"Tuftella!" she bleated as she reached the very edge. "We have come to save you!" And she hurled herself into thin air.

11
Bungee...!

S al had realized—a little too late—that the sobbing and sighing wasn't sobbing and sighing at all. It was the anxious cries of humans, looking up at her from the riverbank far below. But now her world was turned upside down.

Sal's eyes bulged, her nostrils flared, and a roaring sound filled her ears. Rushing air flattened her fleece and forced her front legs out sideways. She was plunging headfirst toward the river, her hind legs attached to a very long piece of elastic! She could see the river rushing up to meet her, feel the spray thrown up by the nearby rocks. Then, just as suddenly as she had fallen, she felt a tremendous jerk, and the river was rushing away again. She was still head down, suspended from the elastic bungee rope, but now she was shooting back up toward the top of the tower. Minus her sunglasses.

"Ohmygrassohmygrassohmypoorpoorsal…!" sobbed Jaycey, peering down.

The warriors had heard Sal's cry as she disappeared and were all out on the platform, crowded dangerously close to the edge despite the jumpmaster's attempts to keep them back. Alice was there too, rooted to the spot, surrounded by sheep. And beginning to feel dizzy.

Sal's hind legs in their bungee strapping shot past the warriors' eyes, then, for a brief moment, her face seemed to hover in midair, right next to the platform.

"Hello, dears," she said. Then she was gone again.

Oxo didn't think twice. He rarely thought more than once, and certainly not in a situation like this. "Five for one and one for five!" he roared. And he launched himself from the platform.

As rescues went, it didn't really work.

Oxo's chest hit the bungee rope and he did his best to grip it between his hind legs. He slid down until his bottom made contact with something hard. It was the stiff plastic cone that protected the strapping around Sal's hind legs. It made a very uncomfortable seat but stopped Oxo sliding any farther. He hung on tightly as the rest of the warriors landed just above him and slid down onto his broad shoulders. They scrabbled their hooves in each other's fleeces and wrapped their forelegs around the bungee rope. Jaycey hung on to Links with her teeth. The air whistled up their noses and through their ears as they fell.

"Five for one and one for five!" they shrieked again as they plunged.

The extra weight on the bungee rope made it stretch farther and Sal not only saw the river this time, she felt it too. *Sploosh!* Her head and shoulders dipped right in. But only for a second.

Boing! The bungee cord had reached the limit of its stretchiness. It went taut, then sprang back, and catapulted its clinging load up toward the top of the tower.

Alice was still there, frozen with fear, balancing giddily on the edge of the platform, clinging to the safety rail with one hand.

"Get away from the edge!" the tense jumpmaster called, trying to reach Alice's swaying body. "Move back."

But Alice didn't hear. As Sal shot past again, the hand that had been holding the safety rail lost its grip and she toppled forward.

The four warriors who had their heads the right way

up—Oxo, Links, Jaycey, and Wills—saw Alice's flailing hand as they plunged past on their way down again. Then they felt the jolt on the rope as she caught hold of it just above their heads.

Alice's scream was so loud that even Deidre, who was craning out of the hostel dormitory window, trying to see the tower, heard it.

Alice floundered wildly in midair for a second, holding on to the bungee with only one hand. Then her other hand swung round and she grabbed hold with that too. She felt the rope against her legs and clenched it between her knees. She hung on tightly, shrieking loudly as the river rushed up to meet them all again.

Wills had managed to glance up. "It's the fairy godtingy!" he called down to the others. "Maybe she's come to—"

He didn't finish. With even more weight on it, the elastic rope was stretching even farther. Sal gulped and closed her eyes, ready to be dunked headfirst again. Then her attention switched from her head to her hooves. Her hind legs were slipping from their strap-ping. It was designed for humans with feet that stick out like bars at the end of their legs, but Sal was a sheep with skinny ankles and little hooves. And they were sliding out. She realized she was in for more than a dunking this time. Just a few yards above the river, her hooves slid free of the bungee and she hit the water with a wallop, sinking like a stone.

Boing! Boing! Boing! Without Sal's weight, the bungee flicked up, then down, then whipped from side to side. The rest of the warriors were flung off and, bleating with terror, landed in the river in a volley of splashes.

The bungee rope shot skyward again, with Alice still clinging desperately to it.

"Ohmysalohmysalohmysal..." gabbled Jaycey, paddling hard to keep her head above water. Then Sal's head burst from beneath the surface, right next to her.

"No need to panic, dear," she gasped, blowing water from her nostrils and shaking droplets from her eyes. "All is well..."

"One for five and five for a swim..." yelled Oxo, and he turned toward the riverbank.

Way above their heads, Alice was clinging on to the bungee for dear life. But only with her hands now. Her knees had slipped and her legs were thrusting up and down like a frog's as she tried to regain her grip. She had stopped shrieking but her mouth was still fixed wide open in silent horror.

And then it was over. A second later there was a final shriek as Alice too lost her grip on the bungee rope and she belly flopped into the water with a *whoomph!*

On the riverbank, Shelly and a small group of bystanders had been staring in shock, their eyes switching rapidly between Alice and the sheep. Now, they watched as a rescue boat zoomed from the shore and fished Alice out of the water.

She lay gasping and flapping in the bottom, like a fish that had just been hooked.

"No room for the animals," the helmsman shouted to his mate. "We'll have to come back for them."

The warriors weren't making any headway in their attempts to swim for the riverbank. The current was too strong.

"Best to stop paddling," panted Wills. "Just go with the flow…"

They were swirled out into the center of the wide river and then across toward the far bank, opposite the tower. The current whizzed them along downstream, faster and faster. Some concerned backpackers broke away from the little knot of people beside the tower and ran along the riverbank trying to keep up with them. But human legs were no match for the racing current and one by one they gave up.

• • •

Alice stumbled out of the rescue boat, dripping wet and shaken and sure she was gong to be asked some very awkward questions. She flipped her wet hair out of her eyes and saw the jumpmaster and her assistant and several other official-looking people striding toward her. Alice quickly decided to play dumb. It didn't come easily.

The jumpmaster didn't ask Alice if she was hurt. She merely demanded, "Can I see your ID, ma'am?"

"I'm sorry?" said Alice, with what she hoped was a dazed smile.

"Your identification. I don't believe you're *Almost Human*. You lied to me!"

"Lied to you…?" Alice swayed. "When?" She put her hand to the back of her head and winced. "Oh dear…My head is so painful. I think I must have banged it in the elevator…" She swayed a little more.

"Yeah, right…" The jumpmaster put her face close to Alice's. "Lady, I want to know what you're up to!"

Alice kept up the swaying. "I remember some sheep—in the elevator. They rushed in and squashed me flat against the back…" She closed her eyes and began to pant. "And then…and then…" She looked down at her clothes. "Why am I soaking wet? Ohh…" She sank to the ground in an elegant swoon.

The jumpmaster and the other bungee staff looked down at her.

"Concussion?" asked one.

"If she's concussed, I'm a kiwi," said the jumpmaster. She looked from Alice to the small crowd of people gathering round. "Anyone know who she is?"

Shelly was squeezing through. "Name's Alice Barton. I picked her up in Auckland this morning. And this is her assistant."

A breathless Deidre had just arrived. "Miss Barton, Miss Barton, are you all right?"

She dropped to her knees beside Alice. "Oh, Miss Barton, what *happened*?"

"Chaos happened," said the jumpmaster through clenched teeth. "Mayhem. Attempted sheepicide!"

"Sheepicide?" Deidre looked up, startled.

One of the backpackers who'd run along the river-bank, trying to keep up with the warriors, was racing back now toward the little crowd around Alice. "They got out about half a mile down on the other side," he gasped. "I saw them. All five!"

Alice's mouth twitched when she heard this, but by biting her tongue she managed to remain silent and motionless.

"Oh, thank goodness for that," said Deidre, though she didn't have a clue what was going on.

"Well, there you go," said Shelly briskly to the jump-master. "No harm done. Let's leave it, shall we?

She squatted and put her hands under Alice's arm-pits. "Take her feet, Deidre," she said.

Deidre did as she was told, and between them they carried the dripping woman back to the hostel. Shelly explained briefly what had happened. Or what *she'd* seen of it anyway.

"I did try to tell her the outfit was a bad idea," she puffed, nodding at Alice's ruined clothes.

When they reached the hostel, they hauled Alice up to the second floor, not too worried about her bottom bumping on each step as they climbed. Alice felt every jolt and heard every word, but she gritted her teeth and remained limp and silent.

"Dump her on the floor," said Shelly, dropping Alice's top end. "I'm not hoisting her up to the top bunk."

Once Alice was certain that the jumpmaster hadn't followed, she opened her eyes. "Where am I...?" she asked faintly.

Her performance was worthy of an Oscar. Even the doctor that Shelly called thought it was *possible* that a bang on the head had made her forget the last few hours. He suggested she rest for a while. Alice clambered onto the top bunk and sat propped against the pillows—Deidre's as well as her own—looking pale and weak.

"I'm going down to the kitchen to knock up something to eat," said Shelly, once the doctor had gone. "You want me to bring you a burger?"

Alice wrinkled her nose. "Is that the best you have?" she asked, her normal tone of voice returning.

"Yep. And I don't usually do room service," said Shelly, giving her a sharp look. "Take it or leave it."

Alice shrugged. "OK," she said as if she were doing

Shelly a favor. "And Deidre, poppet, go and find my photograph. It should be ready by now."

"Yes, Miss Barton."

Deidre trotted off to the hut near the tower, the one where Alice had been weighed. There was a display board outside covered with photos. A camera, fixed on a pole beside the river, automatically took shots of everybody the moment they jumped. All the photos were displayed on the board. Deidre scanned the rows of pictures, then stopped. She clamped her hand over her mouth, regained control, paid for the photo, and took it back to the dorm.

"I'm sorry, Miss Barton," she said as she handed it over. "It isn't very, um, flattering…"

Alice glanced at the photograph, then at Deidre, who was squeaking quietly as she struggled to keep a straight face.

"Of course," said Deidre, trying to find something nice to say, "nobody looks their *absolute* best upside down with their mouth wide open and their knees behind their ears…" she tailed off as the laughter bubbled out.

"Deidre, poppet," said Alice quietly. "Shut up." Her

pride was hurt but she was also relieved. She had proof that she had jumped. "Get this emailed to Mr. Creeply. And find out what I have to do next."

The door burst open and Shelly appeared with a tray full of burgers and chips. "Grub up." She grinned and handed a plate of food to Alice. "Don't drop any on your nice white trousers."

"I'm glad you're so easily amused," said Alice, but she took the plate. She was suddenly starving. She was still eating her burger when Deidre looked up from the laptop.

"Mr. Creeply's got the photo," said Deidre. "And accepted it as proof." She paused. "Um, Shelly? D'you happen to know anything about...Tickler's Turnpike?"

"Tickler's Turnpike?" Shelly laughed. "Heck, yes. Now that *will* make your eyes water!"

12
Rose's Ruse

The warriors had followed Wills's advice and "gone with the flow." The banks on either side of the river seemed to flash past in a blur of green, and soon they were a long way downstream from the bungee tower.

"Ohmygrassohmygrassohmypoorpoorhooves…" Jaycey had wailed as she was swept through a series of small, shallow rapids and her dainty hooves scraped the rocks beneath.

A bit farther on, the river began to narrow and the current raced still faster.

"Forget the flow," Oxo had gurgled, trying to talk without getting his mouth full of water. "Swim!" He turned and paddled as hard as he could.

He had spotted a small bay that had been gouged into the nearest riverbank, and seen that the water in the bay was moving more slowly. He'd also seen that Wills and Jaycey were almost exhausted. He paddled harder and harder, then suddenly felt himself being swirled sideways, out of the current, and into the shallow water of the little bay. Sal was swirled in next, then Links. But Wills and Jaycey were too small and too weak to cross the current. It swept them on, past the little bay, toward the next line of rapids.

"Keep paddling!" Oxo shouted to them, then he threw himself back into the current and surged out to the struggling youngsters. He opened his mouth and picked Wills up by the neck, in the way a cat picks up a kitten. "Got goo," he grunted through clenched teeth.

Jaycey used her own teeth to hang on to Oxo's tail and he turned and paddled for the bay. Strong though Oxo was, he couldn't have managed if Links hadn't plunged in to help. Between them, they shoved and dragged the exhausted young sheep until the current suddenly released them all and they were able to stagger onto the beach.

"This way, dears," called Sal from the top of a short, concrete slope. "I think we could all do with a nice rest."

The slope was a slipway in front of a wooden boathouse. A few rubber rafts had been pulled clear of the water and were tied to metal rings fixed into the slope.

Outside the boathouse, there was a rack, neatly stacked with kayaks, and another stacked with paddles. The boathouse door was locked. It was getting late and the humans who worked there had gone home. Only a lone backpacker on the other side of the river saw the bedraggled group of sheep emerge from the water. He whooped with relief, turned, and raced back the way he'd come, back toward the bungee tower to pass on the good news.

The warriors made their way around the side of the boathouse to the grassy bank behind it, led by Oxo's nose.

"All that going with the flow makes you hungry," he said, ripping up a mouthful of grass.

Sal sat down heavily. "Possibly, dear," she said. "But my stomachs don't know which way up they are. I'll just sit and think."

Jaycey and Wills sank to the ground close to Sal, their sides still heaving, their wet fleeces plastered flat against their small bodies.

"Wills, man," said Links. "You is real skinny."

Wills didn't answer. He was already fast asleep. Exhausted.

Jaycey's eyes had also closed.

The older sheep munched on, but for only a short while before they too settled down to dream of barns and home…and maidens in distress.

• • •

It was getting on toward bedtime in Australia too, but Tod and Ida were wide awake and thinking of their little flock of rare breed sheep. In fact, they were getting more and more worried about them.

"Is it too early to Skype Auntie Rose?" Tod asked, looking at the clock on Uncle Frank's kitchen wall.

"Well, if it's supper time here in Australia, then it's breakfast time in England," said Ida. "And no, that's not too early." She sipped her cocoa. "Tod, why am I drinking this? The weather's far too hot for cocoa."

"Because it's good for you, Gran," said Tod. "You need milk to make you grow big and strong. Here, have a dollop of ice cream to cool it down."

He plopped a scoop of ice cream into his gran's mug of cocoa. "Can we borrow your laptop again, please, Uncle Frank?" he asked.

Frank slid it across the table. "I'm one step ahead of you. There's Rose now. Looking fresh as a dandelion."

Rose wasn't feeling as fresh as a dandelion, or a daisy or any other sort of flower. She wasn't feeling fresh at all. She hadn't had a good night's sleep for ages. Not since Ida's sheep had disappeared without trace from her field by the sea.

She *had* stopped worrying that they'd fallen into the harbor and drowned. Their bodies would have been found by now. But that was small comfort. Where were they?

The hardest part was knowing what to say to Ida and Tod when they rang and it was even worse when she used the webcam, like she was doing now, so they could see her as well as speak.

"Hello, Tod. Hello, Frank. Hello, Ida," she shouted at her laptop as soon as she saw them all on her screen. The microphone picked up her voice, and thousands of miles away in Australia, it boomed out of the laptop in her brother Frank's kitchen.

"Hello, Rose," Ida shouted back. "How are you?"

"Fine. Just fine." Rose's voice rattled the clock on Frank's kitchen wall.

"Amazing, isn't it?" said Frank. "This technology malarkey."

"Brilliant," agreed Tod. "Deafening too."

"How are our sheep?" Ida was shouting. "Are you going to let us see them at last?"

"Yes," lied Rose. "I'm taking the laptop out into the field right now." She did so, carefully, and put it down with the web camera facing the fence. "There you are. Can you see them?"

Ida and Tod peered excitedly at their screen.

"Move the camera, please, Auntie Rose," said Tod. "We can only see grass."

"Good," muttered Rose under her breath. She moved the laptop slightly. "Is that any better?"

Tod and Ida peered again. In the distance, against the fence, they could just about make out a few whitish-brown blobs.

"Can you get a bit closer to them, Rose?" asked Ida. "We can't see them clearly."

"No," shouted Rose. "They won't stand still if I get too near." She waited for a few moments, then shouted again, "That's it. I'm going indoors now. I'm getting cold. It's not eighty degrees here, you know. I'll speak to you again soon. Byee." And the laptop snapped shut.

"Oh, well," sighed Ida, as the screen on Frank's

laptop went blank. Then, after a moment, she said, "Tod...Did you think the sheep looked a bit...strange?"

Tod shook his head. "No, Gran."

"No?"

"No. They didn't look like sheep at all."

• • •

Back across the other side of the world, in the chilly autumn breeze at Murkton-on-Sea, Rose was hurrying across to the fence. She bent down and began to pull sheep from the wire. Five paper cutouts, that is, decorated with felt tip and bits of knitting wool.

Rose sighed deeply. She didn't want to ruin their vacation, but was she doing the right thing by keeping the truth from Tod and Ida?

"Lucky it didn't rain," she said to the cutout sheep. "But I can't keep this up for much longer. I'm going to have to tell them the truth."

13
The Lock Picker

While Ida sipped her cocoa and ice cream and wondered what was bothering Rose, Tod and Uncle Frank went out to check that all the rescued animals were safely bedded down for the night.

When they'd finished, Tod stood in the yard, staring up at the beautiful star-spangled night sky. He lowered his head slowly, then stood quite still. He was sure he could see a dim light shining from the window at the very top of the Maiden Tower. It darted about like the beam of a torch. Then suddenly vanished. Had he imagined it?

"Get a move on, mate," said Uncle Frank. "It's a bit late for stargazing."

Tod suddenly felt silly. He *must* have been seeing things. He followed Uncle Frank back to the kitchen. They were soon talking about the Skype call again.

"Rose was always a bit scatterbrained," Frank said.

"But even she can't have lost a whole flock of sheep. Go on, you daft Brits, get to bed, the pair of you."

• • •

The warriors slept soundly all night on the grass beside the Rotapangi River and woke refreshed. As the sun came up, their damp fleeces began to dry properly and they all felt warmer and more comfortable.

"What I don't get, Sal," said Oxo, "is why you hopped off the tower like you were a bird."

"I thought I heard Tuftella calling," said Sal. "But I'm afraid it was only humans."

Jaycey wasn't listening. She was examining one of her hooves. "Just look at this chip," she said crossly. "Look at it. What I need is some polish. Where's our fairy godtingy when I need her?"

No one knew. The last time they'd seen her, she was boinging skyward on the end of a piece of elastic. It was all rather puzzling.

"Well," said Oxo, "there's always one thing you can do when a fairy godtingy's gone missing."

"What?" asked the others.

"Eat breakfast."

• • •

While the sheep hungrily munched juicy grass behind the boathouse, their fairy godtingy was nibbling a slice of burnt toast as she bounced and bumped along in Trevor, Shelly's battered truck.

"Sorry about the charcoal," called Shelly from behind the wheel. "The toaster at the roadhouse has only got two settings. Burnt or very burnt."

Alice didn't reply. She was not enjoying this so-called breakfast and she had not enjoyed a good night's sleep. The other people in the dorm hadn't clipped their toenails on her bunk as the receptionist said they might, but they had certainly talked a lot. And not to her. They had jabbered till the early hours and merely shrugged their shoulders and carried on when she ordered them to shut up. Then, long before dawn, it was zip…zip…rustle, rustle, cough, sneeze, as a couple of girls who were planning to catch an early bus had slipped from their bunks and started packing to leave.

"I'm dead scared about the next place," whispered one of them, unzipping her rucksack for the umpteenth time to stuff in her pj's.

"Me too," whispered her friend, accidentally

dropping her boots on the floor. "They say Tickler's Turnpike is *the* worst one of all."

"Will you be quiet!" yelled Alice, sitting up in her bunk and banging her head on the ceiling. "I am *trying* to sleep!"

"Sorry...sorry..." whispered both girls and they tiptoed from the dorm, attempting, without success, to avoid bumping their rucksacks against the bunks as they passed.

Three sleepless hours later, Alice was still thinking about what the girls had said. She stopped nibbling her burnt toast.

"This Tickler's Turnpike," she said to Shelly. "Is it really that bad?"

"Yeah," laughed Shelly. "Toughest bit of white water in the country. The river gets squeezed between two cliffs and, er...speeds up. But look on the bright side. The photo can't possibly be worse than the bungee one."

It was a very short ride. Shelly had been driving parallel to the river and soon drew up beside a low brick building.

"Here we go," she cried, jumping out. "Rotapangi Rafters."

"But I'm not rafting," objected Alice, still in her seat. "This must be the wrong company."

"This is the *only* company," said Shelly. "They call themselves Rotapangi Rafters but they cover all the white water sports. They've got places up and down the river, both sides..." She stopped and frowned at Alice. "What did you just say? You're not rafting...?"

"You heard me correctly," said Alice.

"So...if you're not rafting, what exactly *are* you planning to do?" Shelly paused. "Tell me you're not kayaking?"

Alice gulped but remained steady. "Those *are* my instructions," she answered stiffly. "Kayak down Tickler's Turnpike."

Shelly whistled long and low. "Well...I guess we'd better find the guys and get you sorted," she said. "And then start praying." She turned to Deidre, who was struggling out of the backseat. "No point in you moving. They don't do doubles. The kayaks here are a strictly solo mode of smashing yourself to pieces."

Alice glared at Shelly, then climbed down from the truck. "You're enjoying this, aren't you?" she said.

"Not as much as you're going to."

Shelly pointed at the front door of the building. "You

book in over there. They'll give you a wet suit, helmet, and life jacket. You'll have to sign a form saying…"

"Don't tell me," said Alice, "That if anything goes wrong, it's not their fault."

"You're getting the hang of this," said Shelly. "Then they're going to ask you if you've done any white water stuff before."

"Of course I haven't," snapped Alice. "Do I look as if I spend my days romping in rivers?"

Shelly shook her head. "No. So you'd better fib. They don't allow first-timers to kayak down Tickler's Turnpike." She pointed at the rocky hillside in front of them. "Anyway, the river's going to take you way down there beyond the bluffs. We'll meet you on the other side."

Alice kept her face very straight when she told the man at the desk that she was experienced in all water sports. And it wasn't entirely untrue. She had once had to do a term's canoeing at school. On a still, shallow lake. She donned the wet suit, rubber socks, life vest, and helmet she was given and handed Shelly the clothes she'd taken off.

"Be careful," she tutted. "You're creasing my cashmere sweater."

Shelly thrust the clothes to Deidre through the truck window, then climbed back into the driving seat. "Good luck!" she called. Then under her breath, "You're gonna need it!"

Deidre leaned out. "Don't worry, Miss Barton. I'll be ready with the camera."

Shelly sat and watched Alice walk away.

"Is it really dangerous?" asked Deidre.

Shelly nodded. "Yeah. It can be. But I guess she'll be all right. If she doesn't fall out." She drove off. "This chunk of land you say she's going to inherit. What's so special about it?"

Deidre shrugged. "I don't know. She's never told me."

Shelly drove around the rocky hillside to another stretch of river and switched off Trevor's engine.

"I suppose she'll be a while yet?" Deidre said. "I think I'll stretch my legs."

She climbed from the truck, taking a couple of small locked bags with her. Shelly spent a while wiping dust and splattered flies from Trevor's windscreen. She glanced at her watch, then wandered off to find Deidre. Alice should be coming through soon and Deidre would be in trouble if she missed taking the photo. Shelly came across Deidre sitting behind a tree. One of the bags was open and papers and maps were spread out on the grass. Deidre was using a bobby pin to swiftly and expertly unlock the second bag.

14
Tickler's Turnpike

Back up river, a young man in shorts and sweatshirt was holding a kayak ready for Alice. She slid herself into the seat and he helped her to fasten the thick plastic apron over her lap, so that from the waist down she was sealed in. Then he handed her a paddle.

"You're sure you're up for it?" he asked. "The Turnpike's no picnic."

Alice stared straight ahead. "Of course," she answered coldly.

The young man shrugged and pushed her off from the bank.

Alice concentrated hard. She felt the river current quicken.

"I can do this…!" she suddenly shouted in an attempt to boost her confidence. Her voice bounced around the rocky cliffs in front of her.

And a lamb heard the echo.

• • •

"It's her!" shouted Wills, excitedly. "The fairy godtingy!"

He had left the other warriors munching breakfast behind the boathouse and was standing on the concrete slipway in front of it. A man had arrived on a motor scooter to unlock the boathouse and was now busy doing something with the rubber rafts. He saw Wills staring at the river and laughed.

"Hiya, fella. What's so interesting?" Then he saw a kayaker in a black wet suit paddling past downstream. "First one today," he said. "She's looking good."

Wills called again, "Guys, guys, come here…"

But the sheep had heard him the first time and were already appearing around the side of the boathouse. They hurried across and stood next to Wills.

The boatman laughed again. "Well, we get all sorts down here," he said. "But I've never had a queue of sheep before." He was untying one of the rubber rafts from the ring that secured it to the concrete slipway, but now he paused.

"I guess I'd better find out where you lot came from." He straightened up, patted Wills on the head, and walked into the boathouse. "Stay right there," he said.

The warriors were staring so hard at the river, they hardly noticed him go.

"Are you sure it's her, dear?" asked Sal. "It doesn't *look* like her."

"Listen!" said Wills urgently. He turned his head to one side to hear better. The others did the same.

"Alice Barton going strong, bound to claim the Billabong…" The voice was loud and clear and undoubtedly belonged to their fairy godtingy. "Bound to claim the Billabong…"

Alice determinedly dipped her paddle from side to side as she chanted, trying to keep her fear at bay. Staring straight ahead, she didn't see the sheep.

"Why does she always turn up at mealtimes?" grumbled Oxo.

"Never mind your stomachs!" cried Sal. "We must follow!"

"Ohmygrass…" bleated Jaycey. "We don't have to get wet *again*, do we? Look at my split ends. *Look* at them…"

But Sal was already intoning.

"A human, strange in word and deed,

Will be their *star* and take the *lead*.
Through foaming waters…"

"Yes, all right," said Oxo. "But we can't *swim* after her."

Wills had looked away to the rubber rafts pulled up on the concrete slipway. He trotted quickly down to the one the boatman had started untying. "Maybe we could all get into this," he called.

The raft was made of thick, red rubber. It was rounded at both ends and had a wide, curved rim all the way round to stop people inside from falling out. There were no forward facing seats, only rubber benches along both sides.

Sal hurried down the slipway and tried to climb in, but her legs were too short. Wills took a little run, then sprang in, and Jaycey followed. She crouched down right in the middle of the raft and buried her face under her front hooves. Links jumped in next before Oxo put his head under Sal's rump and lifted her up and over the rim. She landed with a thud at the back end of the raft, which promptly began to slide down the slope.

"Oh dear, I'm so sorry," said Sal.

"No, no, that's good," cried Wills.

The half-untied rope slipped out of its ring and the raft slithered to the bottom of the slipway and splashed into the little bay. Oxo galloped after it.

"Wait for the leader, then!" He steadied himself, leapt for the raft, and landed heavily next to Sal. The front end of the raft tipped right up in the air and the back end dipped so far down that water sloshed in over the rim.

"Spread out," called Wills, "before we fall out." He managed to clamber forward with Links following.

They shuffled around a bit until the raft felt steady under their hooves. Links and Wills stood on one side, Sal and Jaycey, who'd come out from under her hooves, on the other. Oxo insisted on standing at the front.

Alice's kayak was by now well past the little bay and moving faster. Her voice was fading.

"Alice Barton going strong..."

Behind her, the raft with its crew of sheep bobbed gently up and down, going nowhere. The boatman suddenly appeared in the boathouse doorway and stared in shock.

"Hey, get out of there!" he yelled, and started running down the slipway.

"We've got to make it move," shouted Wills, and he began to rock on his hooves like a dancer. "Rock, everyone! Rock!"

The others copied Wills, rocking their bodies forward and backward.

Links nodded approval. "Hey, nice moves, guys...Now, with the beat." And he began to rap.

"We ain't so daft as it might appear,
An' we's rocking this raft 'cause we can hear
The lady out there and her voice, we know,
Is our fairy godtingy, so we gotta go...
But it sure won't be no laughing matter,
So we's sayin' no, no time for chatter.
So guys just rock,
Rock this raft...Rock this raft,
Don't pitter-patter.
Rock this raft. Rock this raft..."

The other warriors joined in and the raft began to tilt up and down rhythmically. It rocked farther out into the little bay. The boatman splashed after it, yelling for the sheep to stop, but before he could reach it, the raft suddenly span round twice, then shot off down the river, caught and carried along by the swift current.

"Stop rocking!" shouted Wills. "And all sit down!"

The sheep crouched as low as they could. The raft bounced along faster and faster and once more the sheep felt the spray of the Rotapangi River on their fleeces.

"What a splendid way to travel," observed Sal. Then as they got even faster, "Um, Wills dear, do we have any of those things humans use to, er, slow things down a bit?"

"Brakes?"

"Yes, dear."

"No."

"Oh."

The trees beside the river had become a green blur again. The raft was gaining on the kayak, but Alice was completely unaware of what and who was behind her. The crash helmet blocked out most sound, and her eyes were still fixed on the river ahead.

"Alice Barton, going strong, bound to claim the..."

Suddenly, as she rounded a bend, a wall of rock appeared in front of her, like a high dam blocking the river. Halfway across it, splitting the wall of rock from top to bottom, was a narrow gorge. The entire Rotapangi River had no choice but to force its way through this narrow gap. And Alice had no choice either. This was Tickler's Turnpike. And it was sucking her toward its dark mouth.

Even inside her helmet, Alice could hear the echoing roar of tumbling water from within the gorge. Mist billowed out like breath from a giant's jaws. She braced herself and paddled hard into the mist. Soon she was plowing through a curtain of spray. The roar was deafening. The kayak plunged into the gorge and down the furious white slope of churning, racing water. Alice screamed, and her scream seemed to be answered by another noise, even louder.

"Mmmaaaaa…!"

It was coming from behind her. She ducked as something large and wide and red skimmed over the top of her helmet and landed with a flat-bottomed whack on the white water ahead of her. As it landed, its occupants bounced high in the air before dropping back down again: *splat, splat, splat, splat, splat!* The raft careered onward and downward with five sheep onboard. Five *sheep!*

Alice lost her paddle, lost her grip, lost everything.

The kayak bounced off one wall of the gorge, then the other. It turned sideways and rolled over with Alice trapped in her seat. Cold water surged into her mouth and up her nose. Then she was the right way up again, spluttering and gasping, with water streaming down her face. But only for a second. The kayak rolled over again. And it went on rolling and tumbling, like a twig down a storm drain.

Ahead of her, the raft with its heavy load of sheep crashed from side to side but stayed upright. Sal managed a backward glance through the drenching spray.

"Our fairy godtingy seems to be very fond of getting wet," she observed before being hurled against Oxo's bottom.

Then the raft shot out of the lower end of the Turnpike, into the relative calm of a wide pool, before twirling twice and floating onward downriver.

"Good effort!" yelled Shelly. She was on the bank with Deidre, waiting for Alice's kayak. Only after she'd shouted did she realize that the raft was manned by sheep.

"Holy-moly...Is that *them* again...?"

Deidre wasn't looking at the raft. She grabbed Shelly's arm. "Miss Barton made it! Sort of..."

She started snapping away with her camera as the kayak, with Alice still on-board, bounced and slithered out through the foam and ended floating upside down toward the bank. Alice thrashed about and righted herself, gasping and coughing.

"Smile, Miss Barton," called Deidre.

But Alice didn't smile. "Those..." she gargled through a throat full of river water. "Those *sheep!*"

• • •

By now the raft was speeding up again, as the river raced onward. Wills did a quick head count. Nobody had been lost overboard.

Links was the first to speak. "Man, we is awesome," he gasped, shaking his curls out of his eyes. "We flied like woolly birds."

"Er, yes," said Wills, who was now peering back the way they had come. "But we flew a bit too fast..."

They all looked. Their fairy godtingy was in the water far behind them. And there was nothing the warriors could do to get back to her.

15
Mr. Creeply Arrives

Shelly waded into the river, caught hold of Alice's kayak, and hauled her onto the bank before the current could sweep her away again. Deidre rushed forward with a dry towel as Alice climbed out.

"Oh, well done, Miss Barton!"

Alice pushed the towel aside. "Don't well done me…" She was gasping but furious. "What's your game, Deidre?"

"Game, Miss Barton…?" Deidre's eyes widened.

Alice dropped her crash helmet. "Sheep do *not* stow away on boats," she panted, moving closer so that her nose was almost touching Deidre's. "Sheep do *not* bungee jump. Sheep do *not* raft. They're your doing. *You* have brought them here. You're trying to sabotage my claim to Barton's Billabong!"

"Why on earth would I do that?" Deidre stepped back away from the angry, wet face of her employer. "I'm just…a secretary."

Alice stood for a moment glaring at Deidre and breathing deeply to calm herself. Then she stalked off to get changed, kicking the crash helmet as she passed. It rolled down the slope and plopped into the river.

"That'll cost her a few dollars extra," said Shelly, watching it float away. She patted Deidre's shoulder. "She's all keyed up with the kayaking. She'll soon get over it."

They sat and waited in the truck. After a short silence, Shelly asked, "Looked at the photo yet, Miss Secretary?"

There was something of a challenge about the way she said "Miss Secretary," but Deidre pretended not to notice. She shook her head and handed over the camera. Shelly looked at the screen. Her face twitched, then creased, then she burst out laughing.

"Remember I said this couldn't possibly be worse than the bungee shot?" She held out the screen for Deidre to see. "I was wrong."

• • •

At Barton's Billabong, Ida and Tod were getting in a bit of cricket practice.

"Well bowled, Gran," called Tod, as one of her spinners knocked his stumps flying.

"She always was handy with a ball," called Frank. He was cleaning out one of the bird cages. The sanctuary looked after orphaned parrots as well as joeys. "Pity she's no good with a bat."

"I could whack you for six any day," said Ida. She flopped down in the shade. "Phew, it's getting hot already."

"It'll be a bit cooler in Brisbane," said Frank.

"For the test match? I hope so." Ida was fanning her face vigorously with her hanky. "But I'm going to enjoy it whatever."

"Glass of water, Gran?" asked Tod, and he trotted off toward Frank's little house to fetch one.

Nat came out of his own cabin as Tod was passing. He was carrying a bag with bread and fruit in it. "Lunch on the go," he grunted as he strode away. "Tell Frank the solicitor guy phoned. He's arriving this morning. I'll make sure the landing strip's clear."

A short while later, a drone in the sky became a roar, and a speck in the distance became a helicopter. It hovered overhead briefly then slowly descended. The rotor blades sliced the air and the draught swirled up fallen leaves and dust. The helicopter landed with a gentle bump just beyond the perimeter fence, and a short, thin man with a bald head and very pale skin climbed out, clutching a large briefcase. He ducked low and crept from under the whirring blades. Once the helicopter had lifted off and flown away again, the new arrival marched solemnly toward the sanctuary gate, where Frank was waiting.

"G'day, Mr. Creeply. Good to see you again."

Mr. Creeply stalked in without a handshake. "I'm getting to grips with the will," he said grimly. "But there is still much to be done." He made it sound like Frank's fault.

Frank beckoned Ida and Tod to join him.

"This is my sister Ida and her grandson, Tod."

"Oh." Mr. Creeply looked at Tod. "I hope I won't be disturbed. Especially by childish noise."

Tod flushed but was too surprised to answer.

Mr. Creeply took a very large, old-fashioned key from his briefcase. "I shall be in the office if you need me." And he stalked away toward the tower.

Frank hurried after him. Tod and Ida exchanged a look and followed.

"So how long d'you reckon you'll be?" Frank asked,

puffing slightly and wishing he were younger and his bones didn't creak so much.

"As long as it takes," replied Mr. Creeply. "Possibly two weeks."

"Two *weeks*?" Frank had been expecting him to say two hours.

"I shall stay here until the job is done," said Mr. Creeply with a severe stare.

"Right," said Frank, his head reeling. "Right…"

Mr. Creeply teetered across the rope bridge and unfastened the great brass padlock that guarded Maiden Tower. The door creaked open. Frank followed Mr. Creeply inside.

The thick stone walls kept the sunlight out and it was gloomy and cold. In the middle of the floor space, a spiral staircase, enclosed in stone, wound up into the darkness above. A narrow wooden door guarded the entrance to the staircase. It was ajar.

Mr. Creeply tutted and pulled it closed. "I hope nobody's been in here?" he said accusingly to Frank. "My clear instructions were that nothing was to be tampered with until all the legal work is completed. By me alone."

"You must have left it open yourself," said Frank. "Nobody but nobody's been in here since you left after your last visit."

He sounded a bit flustered. And Tod, who'd crept across the rope bridge, was very curious. He remembered the evening he'd seen a light in the topmost window and felt an odd little shiver run down his spine. Was Uncle Frank telling the truth about the staircase door? Why would he lie?

Outside the tower, Tod moved sharply back out of sight as Mr. Creeply turned. There was another door beyond the stone stairwell and the solicitor unlocked this one too and pushed it open. He walked inside, followed by Frank. Tod edged forward again.

"Much going on?"

Tod jumped at the voice behind him. Nat was standing at the other end of the rope bridge.

Tod blushed. "Er, I can't see."

"They're not trying to get up the stairs, are they?" asked Nat.

"No. Through one of the other doors."

"Good. Only the stairs are a nightmare. Too steep and slippery for your poor old uncle." Nat smiled a rare smile. "Though I wouldn't worry too much if a nit-picky solicitor took a tumble." He nodded at Tod before moving away. "They've either gone into the office or the dungeon. I'd guess the office. Don't get your nose caught."

Tod peered into the tower again. Mr. Creeply and Uncle Frank were standing in the office doorway, surveying the room in front of them. It ran right around the tower's ground floor, inside the outer wall. A complete circle, like a hollow tire on a wheel. There was just one window and that let in very little light. The ceiling was made of stout wooden beams and planks, and from it hung a single ancient light bulb. Frank clicked the switch and the bulb lit the nearest part of the office, casting dark shadows beyond.

Mr. Creeply tutted at the enormity of the task ahead. "Did I say two weeks?" he muttered.

The room was littered with untidy piles of paperwork. It was stacked on the floor, on the filing cabinets, on the two chairs, and on the desk.

"There was never enough time to do this sort of stuff," Frank said with a guilty sigh.

Mr. Creeply carefully removed a pile of papers

from a chair, fanned away the dust, and sat down at the desk. "I don't eat much," he said, clicking open his briefcase. "But would appreciate meals here at the desk. I shall sleep here too."

Frank nodded. "Right…" he said. "Right…"

"Please close the door on your way out," added Mr. Creeply.

Frank hesitated, turned, and stomped out, shutting the office door firmly. Tod heard him coming and nipped back across the bridge.

"Well, mate," said Uncle Frank as he joined him. "Did you get a good look?"

Tod blushed scarlet again. "Er…"

Uncle Frank laughed. "That rope bridge is a dead giveaway. You set it swinging like a pendulum on a clock." He ruffled Tod's hair. "I can smell the curry your Gran's cooking for lunch. Let's forget solicitors and get the fire hoses out."

As they strode back to the house, Tod suddenly remembered a question he'd been meaning to ask for some time. "Uncle Frank…supposing Alice Barton doesn't complete the challenges Motte and Bailey set for her? What will happen to the sanctuary and everything then?"

Frank shrugged. "If that happens, mate, it all comes to me."

16
Bubble-Bubble

Still in their raft on the Rotapangi River, the warriors were also becoming aware of a smell. And it wasn't curry. With their fairy godtingy left far behind, they were floating helplessly on. But the river was getting wider. They could no longer see the banks on either side.

"I think," said Wills, "it's become a lake. That's sort of bigger than a pond but smaller than the ocean."

"Much smaller than the ocean, dear," said Sal, who had very good eyesight. "I can see land. There, look."

The sheep peered ahead over the rim of the raft.

"Is that what stinks?" asked Oxo.

They soon found out. The raft drifted across the lake and ran aground on a small beach, where the smell hung like a haze in the air.

"Phaw…" said Links, wrinkling his nose. "It's like that time Tod forgot to collect the eggs and they all went rotten, right?"

"And what's that funny noise?" asked Oxo suddenly. He scanned the beach, ready for action.

They all clambered from the raft and stood listening.

Bubble…Bubble…Plop…Bubble…Plop…Splat… Splash…Bubble…Bubble…

"Ohmygrassohymgrass…" whispered Jaycey. "What *is* that?"

"Better check it out," said Oxo. He boldly led the way toward a narrow path on the far side of the beach.

The warriors walked in single file along the path, which wound through the strangest landscape they'd ever seen. The ground was completely flat and vividly colorful, as if great pots of paint had been knocked over and the paints had mixed together. Yellows ran into greens, which ran into reds and into blacks. A white salty film covered some areas, turning the reds pink. Nothing grew, not a single blade of grass. But weirdest of all were the bubbling pools of gray mud that were making the noise.

"Stick to the path," said Wills. "Those pools look really hot."

"But we *are* going the right way, dear," Sal called excitedly from the back of the line. "Remember:

"Through foaming waters, Outback dire,
Through thirst and famine, *mud and mire…*"

"They forgot to mention the mud was boiling, man,"
said Links.

"And stinking," added Oxo.

"Keep going and stick to the path," said Wills.

• • •

Shelly told Alice about the amazing mud pools of
Wanageeki and Alice listened carefully. She was in dry
clothes now, sitting in Trevor at Tickler's Turnpike. She
was still deeply suspicious about the sheep but had
decided it was ridiculous to blame Deidre. Nevertheless,
she was bruised and aching all over, which was why
Shelly was telling her about the mud pools. They were
apparently "top banana" in the soothing and pampering stakes, and Alice longed for a bit of pampering.

"So have you got time to give it a go, d'you reckon?"
asked Shelly.

As if on cue, the laptop on Deidre's knees pinged as
an email came in. Deidre looked at it.

"From Mr. Creeply," she said. "He's accepted the
Turnpike photo."

"So very generous," snorted Alice.

"And he's giving details of the next challenge…"
Deidre read silently, then, "Oh."

"Shark wrestling?" asked Alice.

"No—not at all…Might even be nice. You've got to
get to Australia first," Deidre said. "To Brisbane."

"What for?"

Deidre swiveled the laptop screen toward Alice.
"Details by Thursday. That's when you have to be at
the Gabba."

"The what?" asked Alice sharply.

"The Gabba?" said Shelly. "That's the Brisbane
Cricket Ground. And Thursday's the first day of the
test match."

17
Merino Geyser

Shelly gave Alice a geography lesson as she drove the few miles from Tickler's Turnpike. "Wanageeki's one of the few places in the world where the Earth's crust is so thin that hot water or mud can bubble straight out of cracks in the ground," she told her proudly. "It's a natural phenomenon."

Alice wasn't interested. She just wanted to get there.

"There are hundreds of baths," Shelly went on. "They're built over the bubbling cracks. Some as big as swimming pools, some as small as bath tubs. Some crystal clear, others milky yellow. And some of the best aren't water at all. They're the ones full of the hot, plopping mud."

Alice yawned. "So where do I get my ticket?"

Shelly parked by the Wanageeki Pools Complex. "Right here," she said.

• • •

On the other side of the little town, the Warrior Sheep had finally picked their way past the bubbling mud pools closest to the lake. The ground had gradually got softer under their hooves and changed from bright red, yellow, and black to green all over.

"Grass!" cried Oxo. "Just when I thought I'd never see it again."

They all grazed hungrily for a while.

"Tastes of rotten eggs, right," mumbled Links.

"I mom't mare," replied Oxo. "Mi'm marving..."

"Ohmygrass...It won't make my breath smell, will it?" asked Jaycey, looking up in alarm. "I mean, you never know who you're going to meet, do you?"

"It'll only be the fairy godtingy," muttered Oxo quietly, so that Sal couldn't hear. "You wait. Half a stomach full and she'll pop up."

But she didn't. And when even Oxo had eaten enough, the sheep wandered on. Every now and then they passed a circle of stony ground on which no grass grew. Some of the circles were surrounded by a low fence.

"Merino Geyser..." Wills read out the words on a sign.

"Merry what, dear?" asked Sal.

"Not merry. Merino." Wills frowned. "I think a Merino's a sort of sheep."

"Dunno," said Oxo. "But a geyser's a guy. Everyone knows that."

"Ooh...So is it pointing the way to some boy sheep?" asked Jaycey. Without waiting for an answer, she trotted off in the direction the sign was pointing. "This needs checking out..." She tossed her head to fluff up her curls. "I bet Down Under guys are *much* better looking than you two."

"No chance," called Oxo.

"Nah, we's the handsomest global, man," said Links.

Jaycey wasn't listening. She slipped under the fence around the circle of rough ground and pirouetted daintily in the center. "And *I'm* so the prettiest."

"Jaycey...!" Wills's cry of alarm came too late.

The earth beneath Jaycey's hooves was beginning to bubble. She looked down in astonishment. The bubbles got bigger and bigger and suddenly they weren't bubbles anymore. They were a jet of water, a jet of water that was getting wider and stronger and hotter and...*Whoosh!*

The geyser burst from the ground right underneath

Jaycey. She shot straight up in the air on top of the column of steaming water and stayed there, her legs paddling helplessly, her cries of shock and fear drowned in the almighty roar.

"Ohmygrassohmygrassohmygrassohmybottom…!"

"So *that's* what a geyser is," murmured Wills, staring in awe.

Three long minutes later, the pressure pushing the geyser out of the ground died away, and the jet of water got smaller and smaller. Jaycey was slowly lowered until she was once more standing in a pool of bubbles. Then they too drained away.

"Ohmygrass…ohymgrass…" she whimpered. Then she added more loudly, "Ohmyfairygodtingy…!"

She stumbled back to join the other astonished sheep, dripping wet and shaking violently.

"There, there, dear…" said Sal, as they huddled round to comfort her.

Oxo couldn't resist it. "See any handsome guys from up there?" he asked.

"N…n…n…no…" Jaycey's teeth were chattering with shock. "B…b…b…but I did see *her*. Our fairy godtingy!"

125

18
Eyes in the Mud

Alice's pampering was going well. She had tried the warm baths and the hot baths. Her hair had been shampooed and her body massaged. Now she was preparing to try the mud bath: guaranteed to make you look ten years younger.

She took off her fluffy white bathrobe and stood on the edge of what looked like an open-air swimming pool. Only it wasn't full of water. It was full of soft, gray mud, which bubbled gently out of the ground, filling the air with its rotten-egg scent.

"You're quite certain the gray will wash off?" Alice said to the bath attendant standing beside her.

"No worries," said the girl, taking Alice's fluffy white bathrobe. "From your skin and your swimsuit."

Alice stepped in and sank down into the warm gloop, feeling it ooze over her body and up to her neck. The bath attendant popped a soft cushion behind her head and gently laid a velvet mask over her face.

"Lie back and enjoy," the girl said. "I'll be back in a while with some chamomile tea."

Alice relaxed. She closed her eyes. "Me Time" was so wonderful. Thursday and Brisbane seemed a long way away. And so did interfering sheep...

On the other side of the fence that surrounded the mud pool, Deidre and Shelly were sitting on the grass, enjoying an ice cream.

"What did you do before?" asked Shelly casually.

"Before what?"

"Joining up with Alice."

"Oh, this and that," said Deidre. "Nothing special."

"And you're really, really *just* a secretary?"

Deidre gave Shelly a look. "I'm not sure what you're getting at. Of course I am."

She handed her cone to Shelly, ending the conversation. "D'you fancy the rest of this? I think I'll shut my eyes for a few minutes."

"Then you're a nosy one," said Shelly, licking the ice cream.

But Deidre didn't answer.

• • •

It had taken Jaycey quite a while to calm down. And to convince her fellow warriors that from the top of the geyser she really had seen their fairy godtingy.

"She was covered in a fluffy white thing," she gasped. "But it was definitely her. And she was standing by a great muddy hole in the ground. And…"

Oxo and Links looked at each other as if she'd gone mad, but Sal set off at a quick trot before Jaycey had even finished.

"She is waiting to guide us again," she called over her shoulder. "Hurry!"

"That'll be guiding us through some more mud and mire, I s'pose," murmured Oxo, pushing past Sal to his rightful place in the lead.

They ran as fast as they could, then skidded to a halt by a large painted sign.

"Another geyser?" asked Oxo.

Wills spelled out the long word "Re-ju-ven-ating… Mud Bath…" He looked at Jaycey. "Is this where…?"

"I can see her!" called Sal excitedly. She was peering through a knothole in the slatted wooden fence. "There! In the mud."

"Ohmygrass! Is she drowning?" asked Jaycey anxiously.

"Out of the way, guys. Ram going through." Oxo lowered his great head and butted the thin fence. The slats were old and his head went straight through with barely a sound. His body followed and he had to dig his hooves in hard to stop himself skidding straight into the mud pool.

The others nipped through the gap and stood uncertainly on the edge. The fairy godtingy was lying up to her neck in mud at the far end. Very still.

"Ohmygrass...Is she dead as well as drowning?" whispered Jaycey.

"Nah...she's just chilling, man..." said Links. He stepped quietly into the pool and sank chest deep in gray mud. "Mmm...Nice..."

The others followed.

"What now?" whispered Wills, who had to stand on tip-hooves to keep his head above the mud.

"We must get closer, of course," said Sal. "She is our guide, remember."

The mud made soft slurping, glugging, plopping noises as the warriors waded slowly through it. They were only a sheep's length away from the fairy godtingy when a droplet of mud got up Sal's nose and made her sneeze. "Ahhhtchoo!"

Alice woke with a fright and sat bolt upright. The mask fell from her face and she found herself staring straight into the yellow eyes of five sheep. *Those* sheep!

She screamed, loud and long. Deidre and Shelly, on the other side of the fence, heard and sprang to their feet.

Shelly came running through the broken fence. "Now what?" she asked.

Attendants were also rushing toward the screaming mud-bather, who had now scrambled from the pool.

"Guys," said Wills, "I think we should, uh, keep a low profile."

The sheep glanced at each other, then sank silently below the surface.

Alice was ranting. "I knew it all along! It's a plot! Get them out of here! Get them *out*!"

Shelly was by her side now. "Get who out?"

"Those *sheep*, of course!" Alice was hysterical.

Shelly and Deidre looked at each other and down at the pool. They could see only bubbles where the sheep had been.

"But, Miss Barton…" said Deidre soothingly. "There *are* no sheep. There's nothing here."

The warriors managed to hold their breath under

the mud until the humans had led a jabbering Alice away to the showers. Then, when everyone had gone, they slipped back out through the gap in the fence.

"Why did she scream like that?" asked Oxo, as they trotted away from the scene of all the noise and fuss.

"We frightened her, man," said Links. "Even fairy godtingys get fright when they're woken up too quick."

"We'd frighten anyone looking like this," moaned Jaycey. "Look at my poor fleece. Look at my hooves. Look at my..."

"I don't suppose," said Wills, before Jaycey could add to the list, "you saw their truck from the top of the geyser? The one they call Trevor?"

Jaycey thought, then shrugged. "Umm...It was over that way, I think." She nodded vaguely in several directions.

"Maybe we should find it and wait for the god-tingy there," Wills suggested. "While she's getting over her fright."

• • •

It took a lot of chamomile tea and concerned attendants bathing her forehead to settle Alice down. And a lot of showering to wash the gray mud off. And a lot of very expensive perfume to mask the smell of bad eggs.

Nobody had mentioned how much that lingered. "Me Time" had been a disaster but Alice was determined to get a grip. The stakes were too high to be frightened off by a bunch of sheep. No matter who was behind them. She strode from the changing room, ready for anything, and with not a hair out of place.

Shelly and Deidre were waiting. Deidre looked worried.

"Right, poppets," said Alice, with a brisk smile. "Brisbane."

"D'you want the good news or the bad news?" asked Shelly.

Alice flinched, but only inwardly. "The bad," she said, still smiling.

"I'm afraid the airport's closed, Miss Barton," said Deidre. "For a week. They're relaying the runway."

"And the good news?"

Deidre wasn't sure if it was good news or not. "Um, Skipper Ed phoned. *Destiny*'s been repaired. He's moored at Rotapangimouth. Awaiting your instructions."

"Where's Rotapangimouth?" asked Alice.

"Mouth of the Rotapangi River, strangely," said Shelly. "About half an hour's drive from here."

"And how long will it take to sail from there to Brisbane?"

"Depends how fast your boat is. Three days?"

Alice counted quickly on her fingers. "Excellent. We'll still be in time. Deidre, phone Captain Ted and tell him we sail today. Then call a taxi." She looked at Shelly. "Trevor is history—except as a luggage wagon. Meet us at the quayside."

Five minutes later, Alice and Deidre were being whisked away in a posh car.

Shelly was quite happy to have Trevor to herself for a bit. She climbed in, made to start the engine, then stopped. And sniffed.

"What the kiwi juice is that?" she said.

She turned and saw five mud-covered sheep blinking at her from the rear seat. Shelly blinked back.

It was a quick journey. Shelly took the back roads and arrived at Rotapangimouth quayside ten minutes before Alice and Deidre.

"Out…" she said, holding Trevor's door open for the warriors. It was an order but Shelly was laughing. "And don't tell her I brought you here. Go on, move." She grinned as the sheep wandered away. "Maybe see you in Oz."

"What'd she say?" asked Oxo.

"See you in Oz," replied Wills. "I think that's the

same as Australia. Which is the other part of Down Under." He stopped and stared. "Look!"

They looked. And saw that they were standing slap bang in front of a large, sleek motor cruiser. The same motor cruiser that had brought them halfway across the world from Murkton-on-Sea.

"It's our Destiny!" they all cried.

"Right," said Wills, bouncing up and down with excitement. "It's *Destiny*!"

The boat's engines were rumbling and Skipper Ed was at the top of the gangway, waiting to welcome Miss Alice Barton back on-board. If welcome was the right word. He didn't notice the five gray, muddy animals on the quayside. Even if he had, he wouldn't have recognized them as the same creatures he'd last seen swimming for their lives in Auckland harbor.

The taxi drew to a halt and Alice stepped out. "Good-bye and good riddance," she said to Trevor as she hurried past him. She smiled at Shelly. "I presume you have something better in Brisbane?"

"I've got Norman," Shelly said. "Want to see a pic?"

"No time," said Alice, who was now at the bottom of the gangway. "Quickly, Deidre."

"Yes, Miss Barton, I'm coming."

Alice bustled up the gangway in a cloud of expensive perfume tinged with bad egg. "Good evening, Captain Ted." She beamed at the skipper. "I have to be in Brisbane as soon as possible. I'm sure you won't let me down."

"Ed..." muttered Ed. "The name's Ed." But Alice didn't hear. Ed signaled his crewmen to cast off the mooring ropes, while his employer leaned on the rail, looking down at the quayside.

"Good-bye, bungee jumps and rafts and mud," she whispered with satisfaction. "And good-bye, shee..." The word became briefly strangled in her throat. She was watching five gray blobs hurrying toward the gangway. "Sheep!" she gasped.

But at the last moment, the gangway was trundled ashore. *Destiny* began to move. A satisfying gap opened between the boat and the quayside, and the sheep were steadily left behind, stranded. Alice watched them as they stood in a forlorn huddle, staring after the boat, bleating sadly.

"Farewell!" she cried. "And may we *never* meet again!"

The warriors saw her standing by the rail. They saw the kisses she blew and her lovely smile, but they couldn't hear a word she said because of a long blast on *Destiny*'s horn.

"I'm sorry, guys," said Oxo, dropping his head. "I should've butted our way on. I didn't know it was going to move so soon."

"It's not your fault, dear." Sal was trying to be brave. "Something will turn up. The Songs of the Fleece are never—"

They all smelled dog at the same moment. And heard a man shouting behind them.

"What's this mob doing loose? Bring 'em on, Gem. Come by! Come by!"

The next moment, the sheep dog was upon the startled warriors, yapping and yelping and driving them away from *Destiny* toward a much bigger boat, a large cargo ship, moored farther along the quay.

The man whistled urgently at the dog and, to escape its snapping teeth, the warriors had no choice. There was only one place to run. They galloped up the wide ramp into the cargo ship's hold.

An iron gate clanged shut behind them.

19
The Chosen Few

The warriors huddled together, their bodies shaking, their heads spinning.

The man with the dog had gone. That was good. There was a man here in the ship but he didn't have a dog. That was even better.

And there were sheep.

One moment the Eppingham rare breeds had been watching their fairy godtingy sail away. The next they were trapped in a ship with a bunch of strangers.

"Guys. Do us a favor, will ya?" Stay down that end. You stink like a sheep-shearer's vest."

It was a large ram speaking on behalf of the other twenty or so ovines. They were all backing away from the warriors, wrinkling their noses.

"No offense," the ram added.

"None taken," said Oxo, standing protectively in front of his own little flock.

He and the other warriors glanced around at the roomy, comfortable pen into which they'd been driven. Actually, it was all right. Better than their little hold on-board *Destiny*. Almost as nice as Ida's barn back in Eppingham. Except that the gate was securely locked. And the ship was now moving.

Oxo turned to the group of stranger sheep again. Apart from the ram, they'd moved as far as they could go against the bars at the far end of the pen.

"So, what's going on here, mate?" Oxo asked, eyeing the other large ram.

"Relocation," said the ram. Then he added pointedly, "For the chosen few."

"Ah…" said Sal. "That will be us. We are all rare breeds. We have often been chosen."

The ram looked disbelievingly at her muddy fleece. "Nice to hear it," he said, though he couldn't think what they might have been chosen for. "Us lot are Merinos, and…"

"Ohmygrass…" wailed Jaycey. "Are you *geysers*? Are you going to whoosh us up in the air any minute now?"

The ram blinked hard. "Erm…No, actually."

Wills had wriggled forward and was standing beside Oxo. "Excuse me," he said politely. "Relocation means moving to live somewhere else, doesn't it?"

"Right," said the ram, relieved to hear a question that made sense. "Our owner in New Zealand has sold us to a farmer in Oz. On account of us Merinos having the finest wool in the world."

"Not!" whispered Jaycey from the safety of Sal's side. "So *not*…"

But Sal was suddenly all aquiver. "Oz?" she gasped. "You mean…Australia?"

The ram backed away slightly. What had he said now? "Sure. Australia. What else?"

"I knew it…" Sal charged across the pen, flakes of gray mud flicking from her fleece, and planted a kiss on the ram's nose.

He was too surprised to move or speak.

"Totally fleeced up!" cried Sal as she ran back to the warriors. "See, all of you! We're on our way to Australia! Our fairy godtingy is *still* guiding us."

Wills wasn't quite sure how she made that out, but what did it matter? They were certainly on a ship going in the right direction.

"High hooves...?" asked Sal, still quivering with excitement.

The warriors each raised a front hoof and clacked them together.

"High hooves!" they cried.

"Big shout out to the fairy godtingy, yo!" added Links.

The Chosen Few looked at each other and shook their heads.

"Crazy Brits," muttered the large ram.

• • •

The journey took three days and in that time the Chosen Few and the warriors got to know each other better. Sal explained about Tuftella, the maiden in distress, and their mission to save her.

"Awesome," the Chosen Few said when she'd finally finished. "That's, er...fantastic." But as soon as she turned away they pulled "crazy Brit" faces at each other.

Jaycey had to admit that the Merino rams were rather handsome, so she hid herself away behind Sal, nibbling frantically at her fleece until she'd got rid of all the gray mud and most of the rotten-egg smell. Then she spent a lot of time polishing her hooves on the straw and fluttering her eyelashes.

• • •

Meanwhile, on-board *Destiny*, the only fluttering being done was by stomachs. *Destiny* was smaller than the cargo ship and it went up and down a lot more. Alice was very ill.

"This is always a rough crossing," Skipper Ed told Deidre. He tried to sound sympathetic. Alice hadn't come out of her cabin for two days, which meant that for two days he hadn't been asked when they were going to arrive. Or been called Ted.

Deidre lurched onward with the bowl of thin soup and slice of dry toast she was taking to Alice. Shelly met her at the cabin door, but as she did so the boat suddenly pitched forward and they both had to grab the rail to stop themselves falling. The soup and toast disappeared over the side.

Shelly grinned at the empty-handed Deidre. "Oh, well," she said. "What doesn't go down can't come up."

Then the cabin door burst open. Alice was standing there, green-tinged and wobbling, but clutching an open laptop. To Shelly's and Deidre's astonishment, she smiled.

"I've just got my instructions for the test match,"

she told them. "Rather unusual. And, of course…" she added, queasy but cheerful, "there won't be any *sheep*."

Then the boat pitched again and she tumbled backward out of sight behind the slamming door.

• • •

The sea around Murkton wasn't at all rough. It was gray and still under a soft, autumn light. In her field above the harbor, Rose was studying a photograph of Ida's five rare breed sheep. It was getting harder and harder to fob Ida off with talk of wonky Skypes. It was time to take the bull by the horns. Or the sheep by the fleece. She looked up at the five very ordinary sheep standing in front of her. She'd borrowed them from a farmer friend.

"Right," muttered Rose. "Let's get started." She put down the photograph, picked up an aerosol can, and advanced on the sheep. "Nothing to be scared of," she said. "This stuff's one hundred percent safe for use on humans *and* animals. And it says the color washes out after one shampoo. Or in your case, one shower of rain. Now. Who's going to be Jaycey?"

20
Maiden Over

It was going to be an exciting day for Tod and Ida. A little plane had arrived very early at the landing strip near Barton's Billabong, and they were clambering aboard.

"Keep your Gran under control, mate," called Frank, waving them off. "And say hello to Brisbane for me."

• • •

The cargo ship was getting close to Brisbane too. Sal had almost finished working her way through the Songs of the Fleece. The Merinos weren't all that keen on her singing but they were politely impressed that she knew so many verses.

"I don't reckon we could manage one between us," said the large ram, whose name was Burl.

"Don't worry about it, bro," said Links. "Try this instead." He tapped his hoof and started nodding.

"You's the Chosen Few from the Kiwi Land,

And that's a weird kinda bird, so we now

   understand.

But you's on the hoof to a new sheep station,

In what you speak of as a relocation.

Relocation to a land called Oz,

And that's real cool, and I'm tellin' you 'cause,

We's headin' there too and you's given us news,

About the bird called emu and the kangaroos.

And though we ain't quite sure what you's

   talkin' about,

You is A1 dudes, so let's give it a shout:

It's been cool to bleat yous…

It's been cool to bleat yous…

It's been cool, cool, cool…cool to bleat yous…"

The other warriors and the Chosen Few joined in, and they were still singing when the ship docked in Brisbane and they were all herded into a truck waiting for them at the quayside.

For one horrible moment, Wills thought the warriors were going to be sent back again, because the truck driver kept peering at a piece of paper and asking why there were twenty-five sheep when he was supposed to pick up only twenty.

"Not our problem," his mate said impatiently. "It's down to the bloke in New Zealand. He's put a zero on the form when he should have put a five."

"S'pose you're right," said the driver. "Stick 'em on and let's go."

The warriors scampered up the ramp after the Chosen Few. The tailgate was bolted behind them and they peered eagerly through the slatted sides of the truck as it made its way from the quayside. They were in Australia! Not that it looked much different from New Zealand yet.

The truck soon came to a halt. It had pulled off the main road. The driver and his mate weren't supposed to stop, but there was something on the radio they didn't want to miss a word of and the reception was suddenly good. They sat on the edge of their seats listening.

"And the tension mounts here at the Gabba..." drawled the radio commentator. "England, having won the toss, are seven for two and in all kinds of trouble..."

The two men in the truck cab sat even farther forward.

In the back, Wills turned to Burl. "Why've we stopped?" he asked.

"Dunno, mate," said Burl. "Can we do your rapping thing one more time?"

So, the warriors and the Chosen Few joined together in singing their "Cool to Bleat Yous" rap again, tapping their hooves noisily on the floor as they sang.

"What's up with them?" the driver asked, glancing round. "Throw 'em some more feed, Brucy. Keep 'em quiet for a bit."

His mate jumped down from the cab, opened the tailgate of the truck, and threw in a bucketful of feed nuts from a bin bolted to the side.

"Hush up, guys, will ya?" he said to the sheep, who were still singing. "We're listening to the match."

"Ripper! Got him!"

Brucy heard the roar from the radio and the equally loud shout from the driver. He dropped the bucket and raced back to the cab. "What happened?" he demanded, scrambling back into his seat.

Wills blinked at the open tailgate and made a decision. He nudged Oxo.

"I think we should get out."

"Out?" said Oxo, snaffling some of the nuts.

"While we've got the chance. We should go now and make our own way."

"Our own way where?" asked Oxo, munching noisily.

"To the maiden in distress, of course."

"Oh, yeah, right," said Oxo. He raised his head and turned to the other warriors. "Time to ship out, sheep. Follow me."

He leapt out and the other rare breeds swiftly followed.

"Good-bye," called Sal to the Merinos.

"Good on ya…" called the Chosen Few. "And good luck…"

The warriors immediately found themselves caught up in a large crowd of hurrying people. They had little choice but to be carried along with the humans. Eventually they reached a broad open gateway in a high wall. From somewhere beyond the gateway, the sheep could hear a voice talking very loudly.

"Well, no more wickets," the voice boomed. "But that's a maiden over."

Sal stopped in her tracks, and the human right behind bumped into her bottom and had to walk round her. Sal had heard a human word she understood.

"Maiden…?" she cried. "Did it say maiden?"

Wills nodded. "Yes. Maiden over."

"What, *knocked* over?" Oxo's chest expanded. "A maiden's being knocked over?"

"Tuftella…" breathed Sal.

"No. Hang on…hang on—" cried Wills.

But he was talking to four pairs of heels.

The sign above the gateway said, *WELCOME TO THE GABBA*, and underneath the sign the milling crowd of humans were showing their tickets and bustling through. Lines of attendants looked at the tickets and only the tickets. They didn't notice five sheep push and shove their way in between the hundreds of human knees and trot quickly up the stone steps to the top of the nearest grandstand.

Oxo couldn't see any maidens being knocked over. He could only see thousands of people, sitting in rows of seats one above the other. They were all looking down, their eyes glued to the vast patch of vivid green grass below. Oxo's tummy rumbled but he spoke sternly to himself. "Don't even think about it, mate. This is no time for grub."

"So, where's tacky Tuftella?" Jaycey asked. "And why are those men in white running about?"

"They're playing cricket," said Wills, who'd often watched it on television with Tod and Ida in the farmhouse kitchen. "That's what I've been trying to tell you. The man with the ball has to throw it at the man with the bat and he tries to hit it then run up and down past the other man with a bat. And if the bowler throws the ball six times and the two batsmen don't run up and down, you say it's a *maiden over*. D'you see...? A maiden..." His voice tailed away amid a great roar of laughter from the crowds around him. The men were still playing cricket but now there was another human running across the grass. A roundish, plum-haired woman in pale pink trousers and top.

Their fairy godtingy!

As the sheep stared, too surprised to move, security guards, in their brightly colored tabards, ran on to the grass after the fairy godtingy. One of them grabbed her arm and she stumbled and fell.

"Oops!" boomed the loudspeaker. "And another maiden over!"

The crowd laughed and groaned but Oxo was already charging down the steps.

"Five for the fairy godtingy!" he roared.

The other warriors hurtled after him. They leapt over the barrier at the bottom of the steps and raced across the grass. The guards had hauled Alice to her feet but a great shout from the crowd made them turn. Astonished, they let go of the pink playing field invader and tried to grab the sheep instead. The warriors scattered and the guards chased them round and round across the outfield, diving after them but never quite catching hold of anything woolly.

Alice gasped in disbelief, then stumbled on and threw herself at the nearest bemused batsman. She planted a kiss on his cheek. Challenge completed! Then two of the guards grasped her arms roughly and she was marched away. Confused by the chasing noisy humans, the sheep lost sight of her.

"Guys…time to ship out!" shouted Oxo, shaking off a guard who had grabbed his tail and racing for the edge of the outfield. The others raced with him.

• • •

In the grandstand, the crowd were loving the show. It was even better than three English batsmen already being out. Deidre's eyes were almost popping out of her head. Shelly nudged her.

"Did you get the picture? Did you get the picture?"

Deidre nodded slowly, still speechless.

And a few rows away, Tod and Ida were also staring dumbly as the sheep, *their* sheep, leapt over the barrier and disappeared, heading for the exit.

"Quick, Tod...!" Ida had finally found her voice. "After them!"

21
Trapped and Lost

Alice was trying her Oscar-winning act again but she wasn't getting any awards. She'd been taken into an office inside the cricket ground and was being severely told off by the Head of Security. There were rules against field invading.

"I'm sooo sorry," simpered Alice.

And rules against kissing batsmen.

"It was very naughty of me," she sobbed.

And then there were the sheep.

"They're not mine," cried Alice in sudden alarm.

"Really?" said the Head of Security. He obviously didn't believe her. "Well, you'll still have to sit here until they've been rounded up."

"No!" Alice jumped to her feet and dashed toward the door.

The Head of Security stepped in front of her and she pushed him over. That was a big mistake.

Deidre was outside the door. It opened and the Head of Security appeared briefly.

"Don't bother waiting," he said. "We'll be filling in paperwork all night."

Then the door slammed again.

Shelly was striding down the corridor toward Deidre.

"Are we good to go?" she asked.

"Er, no," said Deidre. "I think Miss Barton's been arrested."

"Shame," said Shelly, trying not to laugh. "Come and say hello to Norman anyway. I've just been down to the quayside and loaded up."

The cricket ground parking lot was emptying fast now. Bad light had stopped play for the day. A dented, dusty, tangerine-orange truck was standing on its own on the tarmac.

"Norm," said Shelly, "this is Deidre."

Deidre giggled. "He's even worse than the last one,"

"What? Smaller..." said Shelly. "I'll grant you that. He's smaller than Trevor. But look on the bright side. You won't have to share him with the luggage. That's nicely packed in Normette."

"Normette?"

Shelly nodded at the small two-wheeled trailer attached to the back of the truck.

"It looks like a baked-bean can on wheels," said Deidre. "Is all Miss Barton's precious stuff in *that*?"

Shelly nodded. "Safe as the Bank of Australia."

There was a narrow door at the end of the rusty metal tube on wheels. She patted its broken plastic handle and the whole door came off in her hand.

"Oops. It's always doing that..." Shelly propped the door back in place. "No dramas. Only needs a bit of string." She rummaged in her pocket and found some.

While Shelly tied the door back together, Deidre checked her laptop.

"The next challenge has come through," she called. "And hey—it's the very last one! We have to get to a place called Lonely Flats."

"Better go and buy some supplies, then," grunted Shelly.

"Supplies?"

"Food, water, toilet paper...Lonely Flats is way out in the Outback. No corner shops out there." Shelly tugged the door string to test it. "Not even any corners."

• • •

While Alice was trapped inside the cricket ground, the warriors were getting lost in the side streets of Brisbane. They'd escaped from the ground through the nearest exit and kept on running until they were out of breath. They were still very confused. Wills had explained again that maiden overs weren't the same thing as maidens in distress and the others *thought* they understood. But if he was right, why had the fairy godtingy run onto the grass? And why had the men chased her? And where was she now?

"Maybe we should get back to the cricket ground," said Wills. "And look for her there?"

"What?" said Jaycey. "And get chased by those horrid men again?"

"Nice grass though," said Oxo, losing his battle to keep it out of his mind.

"This is not about grass, Oxo," said Sal, giving him one of her looks. "It is about Destiny." She turned to Wills. "Which way do we go, dear?"

Wills gazed around at the maze of roads and buildings. He looked up at the sky but there was no help there. The sun had gone behind clouds. He swallowed hard. He had no idea.

22
No Reply

"Wills…? Oxo…? Jaycey…?"

Tod was getting hoarse and so was Ida. They'd been chasing around Brisbane for hours. Calling, whistling, searching, stopping passersby to ask if anyone had seen a small flock of sheep. There had, in fact, been several sightings near the cricket ground, but nobody knew where they'd gone after that.

Finally, exhausted and hungry, Tod and Ida went to a police station and reported their rare breeds missing. Then they trudged to the little hotel where they were staying the night. "Boy, has that Rose got some explaining to do," growled Ida.

Rose was ready when the call came.

It was extremely early, only just light in Murkton-on-Sea but she was already up and eager. She even spoke first.

"Hello, Ida. How's Brisbane? Hang on a minute…"

She was trying to sound casual as she bustled outdoors, carrying her laptop. She took it into the field and set it on the grass, making sure the little camera was pointing in the right direction. A few seconds later, thousands of miles away in Brisbane, the screen on the hotel computer was showing five assorted sheep, grazing in the gray morning light.

"There," said Rose. "Now, you can say hello to your lovely rare breeds."

Tod and Ida stared at their screen without speaking. The silence was a long one.

Rose began to panic. "Um...I know Links isn't looking quite as curly as usual," she said quickly. "But don't worry—it's only the damp weather."

"Is it?" said Ida, trying to stay calm. "And what about Sal? Why's she looking so thin?"

"Thin?" Rose gulped hard. "She's not thin. Just...not so fat."

"And Jaycey?" Ida was sounding less calm now. "What are those brown blobs all over her fleece?"

"Um..." Rose's voice rose to a dry squeak. "Mud! Yes—she got splashed with mud."

Ida's patience snapped. "I think you mean

157

paint!" She drew a deep breath. "Rose. They are *not* our sheep!"

"Don't be silly, Ida. Of course—"

"*Rose!* Our sheep are *here*. In Brisbane!"

"They're what?"

"They're here. I don't know how, but they are. And now we've lost them again. So you can stop pretending."

The long silence was at the other end now. It was broken by a sniff before Rose spoke in a tiny voice.

"Oh, Ida, I'm so sorry..." The sniff became a full-scale blub.

Ida finally forgave Rose, and in Murkton, Rose finally stopped crying. Both said sorry several times and Tod told them both that everything would be all right. Finally, he logged off from the hotel computer and he and Gran went up to their room. They ate a few leftover sandwiches for supper.

"I think we should phone Uncle Frank before we go to bed," Tod said. "He'll worry if he doesn't hear from us."

So they did. But the phone at Barton's Billabong just rang and rang.

"I expect he's already asleep," said Gran. But they

both knew that Frank never went to bed early. That he would be waiting for their call…

• • •

Tod and Ida woke early next morning. They hadn't slept well. They phoned the police station but nobody had handed in a flock of sheep. They phoned Frank again, but still he didn't answer. Ida chewed her lip, then made a decision.

"We need to get back to the Billabong," she said. "Your Uncle Frank might be ill. And he's more important than the sheep."

Tod swallowed hard but nodded. He knew she was right.

23
Boomer and Jaz

The warriors were completely lost. While Tod and Ida were tossing and turning in their hotel room and Alice was locked in the cricket ground, the sheep had continued to wander, far beyond the suburbs of Brisbane. Still straining their eyes for a sight of their fairy godtingy, and their ears for the sobbing and sighing of Tuftella.

Now, they were in open countryside dotted with trees, and there was food at last, of a kind. Oxo spotted it first.

"Comfort stop," he called, and rumbled wearily toward the patch of rough, prickly grass amid the trees.

The other sheep followed, got their heads down, and munched hungrily. Nobody complained that the stuff was dry and tasteless.

And nobody noticed that they were being watched. Until Jaycey looked up and squealed.

"Ohmygrass...! Looklooklook..."

The others looked. And saw the strangest bunch of creatures staring back at them from across the clearing. Eight or nine of them. They seemed to be mostly made up of feet. And tail. Their tails were so thick and long, they were leaning back on them. Their short, sleek, grayish brown fur gleamed in the dawn sunshine. And one of the females had a little joey peeping from her pocket.

"Kangaroos!" Wills was so excited he forgot about being worried.

"Kangawhat?" asked Oxo.

"Kangaroos. You remember. The Chosen Few on the ship told us about them."

The largest male hopped forward and spoke.

"G'day. You guys just passing through?"

"Yeah," replied Oxo, drawing himself up, ready for trouble. "Just passing through. What of it?"

The kangaroo leaned back. "Nothing. You look lost, that's all." His voice had become slightly cooler.

"Lost? Not me, mate," growled Oxo.

Sal edged in front of him before he could start a fight. "But we *are* a long way from home," she said, and held up a front hoof. "From Eppingham, in fact."

161

The kangaroo looked surprised, but leaned down and touched her hoof with his small front paw.

"Eppingham? That would be near...Sydney?" he guessed.

It was Sal's turn to look surprised. "Er..." she turned to Wills. "Is it, dear?"

Wills was still bouncing with excitement at meeting kangaroos. "No," he laughed. "It's in England."

"Oh, yes, of course," said Sal.

One of the young females tossed her head. "You're fibberooing," she said. "We get busloads of tourists from England and none of them look like you."

The joey piped up, "Are they the ones that go bright red in the sun?"

"Lots of them do, yes, dear," said his mother.

"I'm not fibberooing," said Wills, slightly hurt. "And we're not tourists. We're on a mission." He glanced sideways at Oxo, not wanting to upset him. "And, er, we would appreciate some directions."

Sal took over again. "That's quite right," she said solemnly. "We have been called by the ancient Songs of the Fleece."

The joey giggled and his mother tapped his head. "Shhh..."

"To save poor, sweet Tuftella," continued Sal. "The fairest ewe of all. We believe she's held captive in Maiden Tower. Have you by chance heard of such a place?"

The kangaroos looked at each other.

"Yeah," said another of the females. "We know where you're talking about."

"We do?" said the big male.

"Well, you should, Boomer, y'big banana," said the female. "It's where they took you when your mum died."

"Oh, right…" said Boomer. "Y'mean Barton's Billabong?"

"Right," said the female. "The sticky-up bit in the water's called Maiden Tower."

"I wouldn't know," said Boomer. "I spent all my time there in a pillowcase."

"Is it far from here?" inquired Sal excitedly.

"And does it have snapping monsters?" asked Oxo.

"Yeah, gotta have snappin' monsters, man," said Links.

"Maybe," said Boomer. "I only met koalas and possums. But is it far? Yeah, the Billabong's a heck of a stretch from here."

"We could take 'em as far as Lonely Flats," suggested the female. "Point 'em in the right direction from there."

Boomer nodded. "We could do that, Jaz. Yeah…"

"Well, what're you waiting for then, y'big banana?" asked Jaz. "Lead the way."

"Right," said Boomer. "Right." And he turned and thrust off with his powerful hind legs. Just one bound took him half the length of a soccer field. He turned and looked back. "You coming or what?" he called.

The warriors gulped and galloped after him, with Jaz and the rest of the kangaroos for company.

"This is so wonderfully kind of you," gasped Sal. "We've lost our fairy godtingy, you see."

"Crazy Brits," squeaked the joey.

His mother tapped his head again, a bit more sharply this time.

24
The Bunyip

Back in Brisbane, Alice had been released with several warnings.

"Crazy Brits," muttered the Head of Security as he set her loose on the world again.

Deidre and Shelly were waiting. So were Norm and Normette. Alice pretended not to notice their resemblance to rusty baked-bean cans. She'd lost a whole night and was in a hurry.

"The last challenge?" she cried, when Deidre showed her the instructions on the laptop. "Well *done*, poppet." Then she frowned suspiciously. "So what exactly is Lonely Flats?"

"Start of the Jumpup Trail," replied Shelly as Norman coughed into life.

"Trail...?" Alice's frown deepened. "Does that imply walking?"

"Not half," said Shelly. "Miles of the stuff."

• • •

Lonely Flats turned out to be just that. Lonely. And flat.

As Norman trundled to a halt and Alice climbed stiffly out, a tall, thin man strolled toward her from a long, low building at the side of the dirt road. The only building. Nothingness stretched beyond it. It was almost sunset.

"You're a bit late," said the man, stretching out his hand. He was wearing jeans and a loose long-sleeved shirt. A baseball cap shaded his dark-skinned face.

Alice managed a smile and shook his hand. "Yes," she said tersely. "The engine of our so-called vehicle overheated, wouldn't you know. And we had to wait for it to cool down." She shot an angry glance at Shelly, who was now standing beside the troublesome Norm. "And you are...?"

"The name's Jon," said the man. "Motte and Bailey were old mates of mine. I promised them I'd get you started safely on the trail." He pointed into the sunset. "The beginning's marked. You turn off this dirt road about twenty minutes down. From there, it should take you about twelve hours to get to Jumpup Crossing." He held up a smallish rucksack. "You're supposed to make do with bush tucker. But I'd be happier if you took an emergency food ration. We needn't tell Mr. Creeply."

"Bush tucker?" Alice was already jolted by the prospect of a twelve-hour walk.

Jon smiled. "Berries, nuts. There's a chart showing which ones are poisonous. If you're lucky, you might catch a lizard or two. And if you're *very* lucky, you might even manage to dig up a few witchetty grubs."

Alice went paler still. Shelly's grin was as big as a slice of melon.

Jon put down the rucksack and picked up a roll of khaki canvas from beside it. "I think you should take a swag too. Keeps the mossies off, if nothing else." He flicked his wrist and the canvas unrolled.

Alice stared in horror at the stiff sleeping bag now spread out on the dirt.

"No tent?" she asked faintly.

Shelly was quivering with silent laughter. "No tent," she chortled. "Just the swag. In the open. Under the stars."

"The most important thing to remember about using a swag," said Jon, "is to check before you get into it." He squatted down and unzipped the side of the canvas bag, then, pulling his shirtsleeve down over his hand, so no skin was left uncovered, he put his arm into the swag and felt around. "Any number of things could have snuck in: spiders—some of them are poisonous. Snakes…"

Alice was rigid.

Jon straightened up and smiled at her again. "It's OK now but if you decide to use it, check again before you get in."

He helped Alice put on the rucksack, while Shelly re-rolled the swag.

"My advice, though, would be to walk through the night. It's cooler."

Alice gulped and stared at him.

"You'll be fine." Jon smiled encouragingly. "That way." He pointed again.

Alice started walking.

"Watch out for the Bunyip," Shelly called.

"The what…?" Alice turned.

"The Bunyip. It hangs out in the bush. Especially around creeks and billabongs. A real nasty beast."

Jon frowned at Shelly.

"Ignore her," he called. "The Bunyip's just one of our Aboriginal legends. A myth. Like your Loch Ness

Monster? And this young lady is very naughty for mentioning it."

Alice didn't thank Jon for his kind words. She glared at Shelly, then stumbled off under the slight but unfamiliar weight of the rucksack on her back.

"Sorry," said Shelly. "I shouldn't have said that." She stood looking guilty for a moment, then grinned. "Any chance of a ginger beer?"

• • •

The humans were still indoors drinking ginger beer when Boomer and Jaz and their mob of kangaroos bounced into Lonely Flats, accompanied by a small flock of panting sheep.

"There y'go," said Boomer. "The trail shoots through to Jumpup Crossing, and Barton's Billabong is just a coupla bounces away from there."

"Respect," said Links. And he led a high hooves and paws with the kangaroos.

"Hey, just watch out for salties," Boomer called as the kangaroos bounced away. "There's still a few around after the floods."

"Watch out for what?" asked Oxo, when the kangaroos had disappeared into the bush.

"Er, salties," said Wills. "I've no idea what they are."

Sal wasn't listening. She was peering into the distance along the Jumpup Trail. "Is it just my eyes," she asked in a hushed voice. "Or can I see our fairy godtingy...?"

The warriors stared. It was getting dark, but they could all see a short, plump human plodding away along the track in front of them. The human disappeared round a bend.

"After her!" shouted Oxo.

They'd almost caught up when Links slowed down.

"Not so noisy," he warned. "*We* don't think we's scary, but 'member how she jumped out of the mud bath ting when she see'd us?"

"How very wise," said Sal. "It's easy to forget how imposing we rare breeds must look to others. We must not overwhelm her this time..."

They hurried forward again, on tip-hooves, making hardly any sound on the soft, red dirt of the track. Soon, there was only a short gap between themselves and the fairy godtingy.

Alice glanced up. Evening had quickly turned to night. She had never seen so many stars. But she didn't stop to wonder at their beauty. She found the sharp, white starlight even more scary than total darkness, and she jumped every time she saw the smallest shadow on the trail. She walked more quickly.

Then she heard it. A sound like breathing, close behind her. Could it be...? She hesitated, then walked faster still. The sound of breathing stayed right behind her. She told herself to stop panicking. The Bunyip didn't exist. It was a myth. She stopped. The breathing was still close. Very, very close. She turned slowly.

And saw ten yellow eyes staring at her!

"Aaaarggghhh!" Alice screamed loudly, turned, and ran.

"She did it again," groaned Links. "Even though we's softly softly…"

"Yeah. How are we s'posed to stick to her side if she keeps running away?" asked Oxo.

"Not only *that*," said Jaycey, before Sal could speak. "If she's supposed to be leading us to tacky Tuftella, how come we haven't heard any sobbing and sighing in *ages*?" She turned and glared at Wills. "Maybe you got it all wrong about the fairy godtingy!"

Wills hung his head. She had a point. As far as he could remember, the fairy godmothers in Tod's books never screamed and ran away. He looked up sadly. "Maybe I did," he said quietly.

"Ohmygrass!" Jaycey tossed her head. "So now you're saying I've been soaked, bounced, boiled, and baked for *nothing*?"

Sal suddenly stamped a hoof. "Oh, for Aries's sake, Jaycey! Wills was *not* wrong. *And* our fairy godtingy is *leading* us. There is nothing in the Songs of the Fleece that says she has to stop for a chat!"

There was an uncomfortable silence, as there always was when Sal got annoyed.

"Are we going to give up now?" she demanded. "Having traveled so far? Farther than any of our kind have traveled in the history of sheepdom?"

The silence became more uncomfortable still.

"No," said Sal. "We are not. Onward, rare breeds!"

So onward they went.

• • •

After her first scream, Alice had run until she'd tripped over. And when she'd turned for another fearful look over her shoulder, the Bunyip's yellow eyes were still staring at her. All ten of them. She dived off the trail, stumbled a few paces, then threw her swag in among the knee-high spiky grass. There was nowhere else to hide. She unzipped the swag with trembling fingers, wriggled in feet first, then yanked the zip right up again so that only the very top of her head was showing. She forgot everything Jon had said about checking inside.

• • •

A short while later, the Warrior Sheep trotted by. They didn't notice the long, browny-green tube lying in the grass. If Oxo had seen it, he might have tried it for taste, but he didn't and the warriors hurried on. And on.

"Ohmyhooves…!" Jaycey sat down abruptly. "I'm soooo tired. Can't we stop, Sal? Please?"

Sal squinted ahead into the darkness. She was surprised, and secretly a little worried that they hadn't caught up with the fairy godtingy again. But Jaycey did look tired. They all were. What with one thing and another, they'd had hardly any sleep since arriving in Australia.

"Forty winks then," she said kindly.

They found a patch of not-too-scratchy grass and, by trampling it as they turned round and round a few times, made a fairly nice place to lie.

"Only forty winks, remember," said Sal, sagging on to her large, comfy rump.

The others were already snoring.

They didn't hear the soft footfall in the bush nearby.

25
The Jumpup Trail

Tod and Ida had spent the day waiting at the airport. They'd forgotten there was only one plane a day from Brisbane to Barton's Billabong and it was dark by the time they arrived back.

Tod glanced up at the tower, remembering the light he thought he'd seen there a few nights earlier. But then a really bright beam of light suddenly shone in their eyes, blinding them for a moment.

"Who's there?" demanded a voice. Nat lowered his torch. "Oh, it's only you guys."

Tod forgot the light in the tower.

"We've been trying to phone my brother," said Ida. "Is he all right?"

"I dunno," said Nat. "I've been looking for him all day. He's not in his house. I was just going to call you."

"Have you asked Mr. Creeply?" said Tod.

Nat nodded. "Yeah. But he never comes out of

his office so he's hardly likely to know." He suddenly patted Ida's arm. "Don't look so worried. I'll bet a fistful of dollars he's had a phone call about an injured joey and gone off to pick it up."

"Without telling anyone?" asked Ida, disbelievingly.

"Wouldn't be the first time," replied Nat. "He's not used to having people around, remember." He gave Ida a brief smile. "If he doesn't turn up in the morning, we'll get the police to go look for him."

• • •

At daybreak on the Jumpup Trail, Alice was wondering if she dared get out of her swag. She'd lain awake most of the night, too scared to move, but as the darkness gave way to dawn, she knew she had to. There was a long way to go to Jumpup Crossing and her time was running out. She peeped fearfully from her swag. No yellow eyes. No Bunyip.

Alice wriggled out and looked around. Nothing! Just endless nothing. But at least it wasn't dark anymore. She ate her meager emergency rations in one go and tossed the empty rucksack away. Then she looked down at the grubby swag she'd sweated in all night, felt a surge of anger, and kicked it hard. A black, hairy leg, about as long as her longest finger, emerged from inside. Then another leg. Then six more as a humongous spider crawled out. It was black and orange and the size of a dinner plate. It paused for a moment as if blinking in the light, then scuttled straight toward Alice's feet.

Her scream would have terrified a busload of Bunyips.

• • •

The warriors had exceeded their forty winks by several thousand. But they all sprang awake as the human scream shattered the Outback silence.

"Whassat?" Oxo was first to his feet, head raised in readiness.

Then he blinked. The sheep were not alone.

Oxo was staring at the bony knees of a creature that was silently towering over them. Looking up, he saw, on top of the long thin legs, a roundish body covered in shaggy gray feathers. And above that was a long gray neck, topped by a small head from which amber-colored eyes bulged.

The creature made no sound. Then, suddenly, it reached out its neck and jabbed a sharp, yellow beak into Oxo's chest.

"Oi—watch it!" Oxo was so surprised, he took a step backward; something he rarely did.

"Ohmygrass..." whimpered Jaycey, cowering next to Sal. "What kind of bird is *that*?" She was guessing it was a bird. She couldn't think of anything else that had two legs and a beak. Even Wills didn't know.

"The big, ugly kind," grunted Oxo, recovering from his surprise.

"Ugly? You ever looked in a pool of water, mate?" The creature cocked its head to one side and regarded Oxo with its bright, amber eye. "What are *you*, anyway? Some kind of woolly kangaroo?" Then, without waiting for an answer, it darted forward and prodded Oxo's chest again with its yellow beak. This was fun. The best since it had dared to prod a wombat.

"Oi! I warned you!" Oxo spluttered.

The bird drew its neck back and bobbed its head. "Just curious," it said. "We get some weird lookin' creatures around here but I never saw one like you before."

"Yeah, well, curiosity killed the cat," growled Oxo.

"It never killed an emu, though." The bird fluffed its feathers and ducked its head cheekily, pretending to jab Oxo again.

Oxo glared at it. "Hit me one more time and you'll be the first!"

Links thrust out his curly chest. It was time to give Oxo some support. "You'd better listen to what he says, man. Show some respect. We is warriors."

The long, gray, feathery neck suddenly shot out and Links felt the iron-hard beak jab into his own shoulder.

"Oops," tittered the emu. "Sorry."

"Hey…" Links staggered back a few steps.

"OK, stick legs," roared Oxo. "If it's a fight you want!" He reversed rapidly for a run-up, lowered his great head, and charged.

The emu skipped out of the way. "Call that a charge?" he inquired, as Oxo skidded past. "I've seen dead dingoes move quicker."

"I said show some respect, man!" shouted Links, and he too lowered his head.

This was more like it. The emu had them both going now. It darted its head one more time, turned, and waggled its bottom at the sheep. Then ran, bounding away, swiftly and effortlessly, its long legs, with their powerful three-toed feet, covering the ground with huge strides.

Oxo and Links hurtled in pursuit, their heads down, their hooves pounding the dusty dirt track.

Sal, Jaycey, and Wills looked at each other.

"I sometimes wish…" sighed Sal. But there was no time to ask exactly what. If they stayed where they were, they would lose Oxo and Links. They raced after the big rams as fast as they could.

26
Wind in the Wires

Jumpup wasn't the biggest place in Australia. The trail from Lonely Flats led into it at one end and a dirt road to nowhere in particular led out of it at the other. In between was just one street with a few houses. The ten people who lived there all knew Jon at Lonely Flats and he'd asked them to take a photograph of Alice Barton when she arrived. This was about as exciting as things ever got in Jumpup and everyone was on the lookout.

"I see dust!" someone shouted. "She's coming!"

Two other residents stretched a green ribbon between two small gum trees on either side of the track expectantly.

Tension mounted. Then an emu appeared at speed. Pursued by a bunch of sheep. The emu ducked under the green ribbon, then swerved off the track into the scrubby bush.

"See ya!" it called over its shoulder as it disappeared. "Not bad for a bunch of overweight woolbags."

"You'd better keep running, mate…" Oxo gasped, his sides heaving. "We're not even up to half speed yet…" He collapsed in a heap. The other warriors flopped beside him.

The watching humans had observed the sheep's arrival with interest.

"Never know what's gonna happen next in Jumpup," said one.

Everyone agreed. It was too hot to argue. They all settled back in the shade and resumed waiting.

The sheep, having got their breath back, hurried under the green ribbon, then along the street, now earnestly looking for their fairy godtingy. There was no sign of her.

"Maybe we passed her on the track just now," suggested Wills. "I couldn't see anything for dust."

"Yeah," agreed Links. "An' we *was* movin' sheeply quick."

They wandered down the street until they reached the last house, then gazed in silence at the vast expanse of nothingness beyond. They all felt very tiny.

"Our fairy godtingy is soooo not here!" Jaycey suddenly sobbed. "Sal, I'm frightened..."

"We's one hundred percent lost this time, man," said Links.

Sal tried to think of something comforting to say but couldn't. "I can't imagine where we went wrong, dears," she sighed finally.

Wills did a bit better. "Well, this *must* be Jumpup Crossing," he said positively. "And Boomer told us Barton's Billabong was just a couple of bounces away from here."

"Yeah, right," grunted Oxo. "But which way are we s'posed to bounce?"

They all stood in anxious, uncomfortable silence again. Links was the first to raise his head. "Listen up, guys," he said softly.

They all listened. And way above their heads, they heard a sort of sobbing and sighing and tap tap tapping.

"It's her again, right?" whispered Links. "The maiden in diswhatsit..."

The sheep were standing at the bottom of a tall wooden pole. Beyond it, they could see another pole, then another and another, and another, a straight line of them, stretching into the endless distance. And the sobbing and sighing was growing louder and louder. It became a wail. A heartrending wail.

"Ohmygrass…" whimpered Jaycey. "It *is* her. Tacky Tuftella…She must be very close…"

Sal drew a deep breath. "Thank you, fairy god-tingy!" she cried. "Wherever you are. I understand. You have guided us thus far, and now we must go on alone. We will follow the sobbing and sighing until we rescue Tuftella from the clutches of evil. Or perish in the attempt! Onward, warriors!"

"Er, Sal…" Wills didn't want to upset her again but he was worried about the poles. They were joined to each other at the top by wires, just like the telephone poles at home in Eppingham. Surely the moaning and wailing was only the breeze in the wires?

Then, as he turned to face Sal, he noticed a wooden board screwed to the side of the last house in Jumpup. On the board was an arrow pointing in the same direction as the poles. And in peeling paint beneath the arrow were the words: BARTON'S BILLABONG ANIMAL SANCTUARY.

"What is it now, dear?" asked Sal, slightly irritably.

"Are you going to tell us the sound we hear is just wind in the wires? As you suggested about the boats at Murkton?"

"No," said Wills. He grinned. "Everything's fine. I was just going to say we're on the right track."

"Oh," said Sal. She beamed. "Excellent." And she set off at a brisk trot. "Wasn't there something we had to watch out for, dear? Something to do with floods...?"

"Salties," said Wills. But he still didn't know what they were.

27
Searching for Frank

The warriors were well on their way toward Barton's Billabong when Alice finally staggered up to the green ribbon.

The good people of Jumpup greeted her most enthusiastically, cameras at the ready.

"Good on you!" said one of the women, handing her a bottle of water. Alice grabbed it and emptied it in one long swig.

"I guess you're hungry too?" the woman went on. She kept her face straight as she handed a little dish to Alice. "We'd be honored if you'd try one of our traditional delicacies."

Alice, who was indeed very hungry, grabbed the dish without a thank you, picked up what she thought was a small, white sausage and stuffed it in her mouth. The taste and the texture were odd. She looked at the woman suspiciously.

"Just witchetty grubs!" said the woman with an

innocent smile. She showed Alice another one. It squirmed in the palm of her hand.

Alice's eyes bulged. She tried to spit the grub out but it was at the back of her throat and going down. Gulp! She shut her eyes and swallowed.

"*Click...click...click...*" went the cameras.

"Sorry about that," gurgled the woman. "Just Motte and Bailey's little joke. They used to love witchetties."

Alice snatched the camera that was held out for her and glanced at the screen. Her face was a picture. Of horror. Again. But this was the final time. The last laugh would not be on her.

She looked up as Norman wheezed into town.

"Oh, well done again, Miss Barton," said Deidre, leaning out of the truck.

Alice could tell she was trying not to laugh. Still, that was another pleasure to look forward to: giving Deidre Dishcloth the sack.

"Here, poppet," she said briskly, thrusting the camera at her. "Email this to Mr. Creeply and let's go. Time's running out."

She climbed into the truck and flopped into a seat. Just a few more hours and success would be hers.

• • •

In the dimly lit office at the base of Maiden Tower, Mr. Creeply's inbox pinged. He smiled at the latest photo and typed a quick reply: "Photo accepted. But I must remind you that the date is November 30 and you must present yourself at Barton's Billabong by sunset today. If you are not here by sunset, the estate will pass to Mr. Frank Smith."

Mr. Creeply smiled again and placed the deeds of ownership to Barton's Billabong neatly on the desk. He didn't for a moment think they'd be going to Mr. Frank Smith.

• • •

Outside the tower, Tod and Ida had completed another search of the sanctuary. Every cage and shelter. Plus two circuits of the perimeter fence.

"I've phoned the police," said Nat, hurrying to join them. "I'll tell you what, though—we could try the creek. Frank occasionally goes fishing there."

He drove them the short distance to the creek in the open-backed van he called an "ute." The creek was about six yards wide and about a yard deep in the middle, with gently sloping banks on either side.

"I'd better get back to watch out for the police," Nat said as he helped Ida out of the ute. "Just keep your eyes open for salties, OK? We had floods recently and there may just be one or two about still. Even this far inland."

Tod's stomach turned over. He knew that salties were saltwater crocodiles: vicious, hungry creatures. And that they were difficult to spot, either in the water or on the bank, because they were the color and texture of the mud and could lie log-still for hours, until something tasty came into range. Then their huge jaws would snap open and their unfortunate victim would be trapped and dragged into the water and held under until it drowned. The biggest salties could easily hold down a small kangaroo or a sheep. Or a human.

Ida felt very sick. Surely Frank couldn't have been dragged in and eaten by a crocodile?

When Nat had driven off, she did something Tod hadn't seen her do for a very long time. She burst into tears.

Tod put his arm around her shoulder.

"Come on, Gran," he said gently. "Frank's too old and leathery for even the hungriest crocodile to bother with."

They searched the bank cautiously, but saw no sign

that anyone had been dragged into the water by a salty. But there was no sign of Frank, either.

"Let's go back, Gran," said Tod at last. "The police should have arrived by now."

But the police were not at the sanctuary when Tod and Ida walked in half an hour later. Nor was Nat. And when Tod tried to telephone the police himself from Frank's house, he found that the wire had been cut.

• • •

And although neither Tod nor Ida had seen a salty, that didn't mean there wasn't one in the creek. Soon after they'd walked away, what they'd imagined to be a large log, lying half submerged in the water, began to move.

28
Snapping Monsters

The warriors had galloped most of the way along the rough track from Jumpup Crossing. They were full of energy after their earlier long sleep, fired up, and ready for anything. They sang as they ran.

"We's the Eppingham Posse
And we's givin' it a go.
We's comin' for Tuftella
If you really wanna know.
She's a special kinda sheep,
She's the fairest ewe of all,
And we's gonna do a rescue
'cause we never fail the call!"

The lone crocodile lay perfectly still, just its eyes visible. Watching. Listening. It had hoped for a snack. Instead, a five-course banquet was trotting its way.

Wills suddenly stopped singing.

"There it is…" he cried excitedly. "Maiden Tower!"

The others stopped and followed his gaze. There, across the creek and a stretch of bush beyond, rose a tall stone building.

"Nice one, Willsyboy…" said Oxo, after they'd all stared at the tower in awed silence for a bit.

Then the great ram glanced at the water between them and their goal. "Last one in's a sissy!" he shouted.

Wills raced after him, then suddenly remembered the kangaroo's warning.

"Whoa! Slow down, Oxo. What was it the kangaroo said about salties? Something to do with floods? That means water…" But he was too late.

Oxo's front hooves were already in the creek when he saw the log move. And noticed the mean greenish-brown eyes staring at him. The salty lunged forward and its great jaws clicked open, revealing rows and rows of sharp teeth. Oxo veered sideways to avoid the teeth but was instantly knocked head-over-hooves by a lash of the croc's great tail. The ram briefly disappeared beneath the frothing brown water. His hooves churned mud from the bottom of the creek as he scrabbled upright, then he slewed this way and that, trying to avoid the snapping jaws and lashing tail. Finally, Oxo gathered all his remaining strength, pushed off, and lunged desperately for the bank. The jaws snapped again. And this time they closed around a part of Oxo's rear end.

"Ohmygrassohmygrassohmyoxooo…!"

Oxo tugged hard, yanking himself free, then scrambled and scrabbled out of the water. The crocodile was left with just a chunk of creamy white fleece in its mouth.

But the danger wasn't over.

"Run!" yelled Wills. "Run. It's coming after us!"

The crocodile wasn't giving up on its dinner easily. It was pulling itself out of the water, its three-meter long body propelled rapidly by its stubby legs and whipping tail.

The warriors turned and fled. Straight into the path of a battered orange truck.

• • •

Deidre, who was taking a turn at driving, jammed on the brakes "It's them again," she gasped. "Those sheep!"

In the passenger seat beside her, Shelly had already seen the crocodile. "Holy-moly!"

Alice leapt up behind her. "I was right all along," she screamed at Deidre. "It *is* a plot. You're using them to stop me getting to the Billabong in time!" She pushed past Shelly, slid the passenger door open, and tried to jump out. She wanted to kick the sheep out of the way, once and for all. But Shelly grabbed her shirt and shoved her back into her seat.

"Idiot!" she said to Alice. "Stupid, stupid idiot!"

Outside the van, the sheep were running in all directions, then reforming into a flock as the crocodile tried to pick out a victim.

"Oh no!" Deidre cried. "It's almost got the little one!"

Shelly opened her door, grasped the edge of Norm's roof, and hauled herself up. She ran along the top, dropped down on to Normette, leaned down, and yanked the door off. String and all. "Glad I never got round to getting that properly fixed," she muttered. Then she stood up and loudly whistled through her fingers. "Here, sheepy sheepy sheep…"

● ● ●

The warriors had veered off the track in an attempt to escape the snapping jaws. Wills heard Shelly and glanced back.

"Guys!" he shouted. "Stop. Turn back!"

In bleating turmoil, the sheep did as he said. They found themselves facing the crocodile's eyes and teeth as it scuttled toward them. But then Links saw what Wills wanted them to do.

"Jump, man, jump!" And he led the way up and through the open doorway of the trailer. Sal, Wills Jaycey, and lastly Oxo followed.

"Drive!" shouted Shelly. "Drive!"

The crocodile's jaws snapped one more time. And were left with just another chunk of Oxo's wool.

"Man," said Links, as the truck and trailer lurched away. "You's gonna be bald by the time we finish Down Under."

Shelly stayed where she was, crouched on Normette's roof, until she was sure the salty had given up the chase. Then she banged on Norm's roof and Deidre pulled up again. Shelly leapt from the roof and swung herself back into the driver's seat.

"They'll make a mess of your luggage," she told Alice cheerfully, "but I'm sure you won't mind that."

"Of course not," replied Alice savagely. "I should *hate* to have them eaten by a crocodile."

Shelly was peering at the creek as she drove, searching for the shallowest stretch. "OK," she warned. "All body parts to be kept inside the vehicle. We're going through."

And she turned Norm down the bank and splashed him into the creek. The water lapped the wheel arches as she drove slowly across.

Peeping out of Normette's open doorway, Jaycey panicked again.

"Ohmygrassohmygrassarethereanymoresalties?"

Oxo grunted. "No worries. Didn't you see my brilliant spin turn?"

"Nah," said Links. "We only see'd you bein' sheared."

Jaycey didn't have to panic for long. Soon, they were on dry land again, bumping toward Barton's Billabong.

Squashed on top of a smart suitcase, Sal was intoning happily:

"And locked in darkest tower tall
Whilst 'neath her snapping monsters crawl…"

"Couldn't get much more snappy than that tingy back there," said Links.

"And did you see who first tried to step out and stand in its path?" inquired Sal. "Who first tried to save us?"

"Our fairy godtingy," they all chorused obediently.

"Quite," said Sal, her eyes gleaming. "And now she carries us to the darkest tower. Now we will face the final thunder!"

The others nodded dutifully. Except for Oxo, who was thoughtfully chewing a toilet paper roll.

• • •

It was while the sheep were dealing with the snapping monster that Tod and Ida had arrived back at the sanctuary and found the phone wire cut and Nat gone missing. For a few moments, they'd stood in Frank's kitchen feeling very alone and vulnerable. There was no mobile reception at the Billabong. All this vast, quiet emptiness, with only themselves and the rescue animals. And Mr. Creeply.

"Is there a phone in the office?" asked Tod suddenly. Ida didn't know.

"I think we need to find out." Tod dropped the end of the phone wire he was holding. "This didn't cut itself. I'm going to speak to Mr. Creeply."

"You're not going without me," Ida told him firmly.

"I've lost my brother and I've lost my lovely flock of sheep. I don't want to lose you too."

"You won't, Gran," said Tod. "But we need to get help quickly."

He gave her a reassuring smile and raced off across the yard.

"Be careful, Tod," Ida shouted after him. "I don't trust that Creeply man." She hitched up her skirt and followed as fast as her old legs would take her.

On reaching the rope bridge, Tod paused in surprise. The tower's main door stood wide open. Tod glanced around, then ran lightly across the bridge.

"Mr. Creeply?" he called, as he reached the tower doorway. There was no answer.

Tod stepped warily into the tower. He blinked as he passed from the bright sunlight into near-darkness. Then the darkness became complete as a pillowcase was thrust over his head.

29
Tuftella

The pillowcase was a long one, the type used as pouches for the joeys. Tod's arms were enclosed, as well as his head, and though he struggled and kicked and wriggled, he couldn't get free. A strong fist shoved him in the back and he stumbled forward. He heard a key turning in a lock, then he was shoved from behind again and felt himself pitching headfirst into space. He bounced painfully on stone steps, then splashed into cold water, and sank like a stone.

Ida wobbled across the rope bridge just as the door inside the tower slammed shut.

"Tod…" she called. "Wait for me…" She couldn't see where Tod had gone. Then, as she walked into the tower, a pillowcase was thrown over her head too.

"Keep still and keep quiet," a voice whispered in her ear. A moment later, she was stumbling against the unseen bottom step of the spiral staircase.

"Lift your feet…" the voice ordered. "Upstairs."

Ida grazed her elbows and shins on the rough stone walls of the staircase as she was jostled upward. Finally, her captor leaned past her and unlocked a door. He shoved her inside, slammed the door behind her, and locked it again.

Outside the door, Nat drew a deep breath. He walked slowly down to the floor just below and stood peering out of the window. Things weren't going entirely to plan. He drummed his fingers on the windowsill as he stared out. Where was she?

Far below in the dungeon, Tod was rolling over and over in the cold water, desperately trying to escape from the pillowcase. It was now soaking wet and clinging to his face. Water had seeped through the fabric and filled his mouth. He was choking and gagging. Drowning!

"It's all right, mate…it's all right…" A bony arm was suddenly under Tod's body, lifting his head and shoulders clear of the water. Then a bony hand grasped the pillowcase and peeled it from Tod's face.

"Uncle Frank!"

• • •

Inside the room at the very top of the tower, Ida tore off her pillowcase hood and found herself face to face with a young woman with pale skin, very long blond hair, and frightened blue eyes. She was holding a small Merino lamb in her arms.

The two women stared at each other.

"Who are you?" they both said in the same breath.

The pale woman opened her mouth to answer, but Ida was already looking desperately around the room. It didn't really matter who this woman was. All that mattered was finding Tod. And Frank.

"I've got to get out of here," she said.

"You can't," the pale woman said. "I've been locked in for weeks."

Ida stared at her a moment more, then ran to the tiny window and peered down. Five floors below, she could see the narrow strip of stone around the base of the tower and the moat surrounding it. She jiggled the iron handle on the window frame. It clearly hadn't been used for years. The circular room contained only a small bed and a table with a plate of half-eaten food. And there was a small three-legged stool.

Ida moved swiftly and picked up the stool. Then smashed it against the window.

"Right…" she said. "Start tying your sheets and blankets together to make a rope. We'll need to rip them up first to make it long enough."

• • •

In the dungeon, Frank and Tod were making their own escape attempt.

Most ancient towers which were surrounded by water had a water gate, and Motte and Bailey had made sure theirs did too. It was guarded by a portcullis: an iron grating that could be wound up or down to let small boats row right into the bottom of the tower.

Since he'd been thrown in the dungeon, Frank had spent hours standing knee-deep in water by the portcullis, using a bit of loose stone to scrape rust and dirt from a wheel fixed to the wall. The wheel was connected to the portcullis. If only he could turn the wheel, he would be able to raise the portcullis and escape.

Now he had Tod to help him, there was a chance they would succeed.

"Are you *sure* it was Nat?" he asked Tod for the umpteenth time as they scraped.

"Sure as I'm standing here with a lump on my head," replied Tod. "I recognized his voice. And his smell: Joeys mixed with aftershave. Didn't you?"

"No, mate. I didn't know a thing. One minute I was sitting in the kitchen waiting for a call from you and your gran, and the next, *Bang!* Woke up in here. Shouted for hours, hoping Mr. Creeply in the office would hear, but these walls just soak up the noise. Motte and Bailey did too good a good job of building their precious Maiden Tower."

• • •

On the fourth floor of the tower, Nat had suddenly straightened up. He could see a battered orange truck coming his way.

"Yes…" he breathed. "At last. This must be her!"

Shelly drove in through the sanctuary gate and pulled up near the house and animal shelters. By the time she'd walked round to the back of Normette, the sheep were out and running off.

Shelly turned with a shrug and a grin at Alice and Deidre.

"Well, here we are, guys. Barton's Billabong. And still an hour till sunset."

But her human passengers were already hurrying away too.

"Yeah, thanks for everything, Shelly," she said to herself brightly. Then answered herself just as cheerfully. "No worries. You're welcome."

The warriors stood at the entrance to the rope bridge, gazing up at the tower.

"We're here, right?" said Links in wonder.

"Yeah. So what's next?" asked Oxo.

"In one of Tod's books," said Wills slowly, "the human maiden in distress was called Rapunzel, and she had very long hair…and she let it hang down and the prince, who was also a warrior, climbed up it and…rescued her. I think."

"Sounds painful, man," said Links. "An' we's not exactly climbing dudes, is it?"

But Sal was ready to burst forth. "Tuftella, Tuftella, let down your fleece!" she cried.

The others looked at each other, then joined in.

"Tuftella, Tuftella, let down your fleece!"

In the room at the top of the tower, Ida looked up sharply from the sheet she was ripping. She hardly dared believe it, but she knew she was right. "Our sheep…" she breathed.

But even her precious and much-loved sheep couldn't distract her for long. She had to escape. She had to find Tod and Frank. She knotted the last two pieces of sheet firmly together.

"Tuftella, Tuftella, let down your…"

The pale woman's pet lamb had been listening. Suddenly, it bleated in reply and leapt on to the windowsill.

Down below, the warriors stopped in mid-call.

"Tuftella!" breathed Sal.

"Mmmm…She's well pretty," said Links.

Oxo nodded in agreement. "Well pretty…"

They all stood gazing up.

"I think she's a Merino," said Wills.

"She's a mess," sniffed Jaycey. "But I thought we were supposed to be rescuing her?"

Oxo pulled himself together. "Right. Yeah."

"And what's more," breathed Sal, "our fairy god-tingy is still with us…We have nothing to fear."

They turned to see their fairy godtingy approaching the rope bridge. She hesitated, then stepped onto it, holding tight to the ropes on either side.

"Follow the fairy godtingy!" shouted Oxo. "One for five and five for Tuftella!"

He charged at the bridge and was on it before he realized the floor wasn't solid. The woven rope was not something a cloven-hoofed animal would normally step on. The others crowded on after him.

"Ohmyhoovesohmyhooves…" squealed Jaycey. "They're going through the holes! Get off this thing! Run!"

The bridge swayed violently from side to side, like a swing boat at a fairground, as the sheep thrashed about, trying not to get their hooves trapped as they scrambled. Ahead of them, Alice lost her grip on the ropes, and with the next downward swoop, she toppled off, splashing into the water below.

"Thank you, thank you," cried Sal as the warriors hurried across. "Even to the last she is sacrificing herself for our sakes."

Nat hadn't seen the fall from the bridge. He'd already left the window on the fourth floor and was running to meet the woman with the plum-colored hair. He was halfway down the stairs of the tower when he met the sheep coming up. For a couple of minutes there was utter confusion. There was no space to push past them and they wouldn't stand still when he tried to climb over them. The plan, he thought to himself, was definitely not going to plan. He finally pushed and shoved past the woolly mass and ran down the rest of the stairs. He stood with his back to the wall and waited, hidden in the shadows. It was going to be OK. She'd arrived. It was time for action.

The warriors continued on up, but it's hard to hurry in tight upward circles on four legs and slippery stone steps. By the time they got to the top, they were all feeling very dizzy.

"Man, I'm spinnin'," puffed Links, staggering against the wall.

"What a shame," said Jaycey sniffily. "I thought you liked being in a spin over tacky Tuftella."

Oxo looked at the heavy door in front of them. They could all hear a sobbing and sighing from the other side. There was plenty of tap tapping too.

"In olden times," said Wills, "they'd use a battering ram."

"Really?" said Oxo. "Look no farther." And he lowered his great head and butted the door hard. It shook and rattled.

Inside the room, the sudden crash made Ida and the pale woman jump in alarm. They were standing by the broken window, tapping out the last sharp pieces of glass. One end of the rope they'd made from sheets and blankets was tied firmly to the leg of the bed and the other end hung down outside the window. They turned briefly to look at the door. "It's not going to hold long," said Ida.

"Just go. Before it's too late," said the young woman. "I'll hold the rope steady and then follow."

Ida climbed out and gripped the rope between her knees.

She began to lower herself down, then remembered she hadn't even found out the woman's name. She paused a moment and called up.

"Who are you?"

"Alice," said the young woman. "I'm Alice Barton."

30
Avaricia

The real Alice Barton turned away from the window as the door finally burst open.

Oxo exploded into the room and skidded to a halt. He was seeing stars and moons and the walls were spinning. "Ouch!" he groaned.

The other warriors crowded in after him.

"Tuftella!" cried Sal.

The pretty lamb they'd seen on the windowsill was in the middle of the floor, staring up at them.

"We have been called by the Songs of the Fleece," continued Sal. "We have traveled from far-away England to save you from distress."

The lamb backed slowly away.

"Crazy Brits," it bleated. Then it jumped into the young woman's arms.

"I told you she wasn't worth it," sniffed Jaycey, and she flounced to the other side of the room.

The others were a bit surprised at Tuftella's reaction, but they'd never rescued a maiden in distress before, so weren't sure what to expect. They gathered around the young woman and tried to coax the lamb to lift its face.

The woman stroked its head gently. "Come on now, Guinevere, don't be silly. They won't hurt you." She stared at the group of sheep who were blinking up at her. "Well," she murmured. "I didn't expect knights in shining fleece."

• • •

Far below, Ida jumped the last few feet to the ground. She hadn't climbed down a rope since she was at school and had been relieved to find that, like riding a bike, it was a skill you don't forget. "Good job she had sheets and blankets and not a duvet…" she muttered as she edged her away around the stone base of the tower. "Couldn't have made much of a rope out of one of them."

• • •

Inside the office, Mr. Creeply was smiling thinly. The chaotic mess that he'd first walked into had been transformed. Papers were stacked in neat piles, tied with tape. The filing cabinets and cupboards were labeled A–Z and the desk was entirely clear except for one box in the middle. It was marked "Deeds to the Property Known as Barton's Billabong."

In front of the desk stood a dripping plumpish woman with a towel wrapped around her shoulders. To one side of the room leaned an equally wet and dripping Shelly, who had dived in and rescued the plumpish woman from the lake. And beside Shelly, stood a very dry-looking Deidre.

Mr. Creeply regarded the expectant, plum-haired lady before him.

"I have to tell you, dear lady," he told her, "that your late uncles Motte and Bailey left their affairs in a considerable mess. And I don't mind admitting that, when I set to work, I feared I would never sort out their paperwork in time for your arrival. But I was prepared for battle, and I was armed with my secret weapon. Shall I let you into my little trick of remaining undisturbed, no matter what is going on around me?" His smile got a little fatter. "Earplugs." He took a pair from his pocket with a flourish and placed them on the desk beside the deed box.

"So." He smiled again. "Congratulations are in order to *both* of us." With another flourish, he spread prints of the unflattering photos across the desk.

The lady in front of him winced but said nothing.

"You have proved yourself a true Down Underer," continued Mr. Creeply. "And your credentials are impeccable."

"Oh no they're not!"

Everyone turned and stared at Ida, who was marching through the doorway. "And I'm here to peck them! That is *not* Miss Alice Barton. The real Alice Barton's been locked at the top of the tower for weeks."

Mr. Creeply's smile suddenly shrank to nothing as a young blond woman carrying a pet lamb appeared behind Ida.

"That's right," said the newcomer. "I'm Alice Barton."

"Holy-moly…" murmured Shelly.

Otherwise there was complete silence for a moment. Then the plum-colored bangs shook slightly and its owner gave a tinkly laugh.

"Don't be ridiculous, poppet. *I* am Alice Barton."

The blond-haired woman shook her head. "No. *I* am." Suddenly firm, she looked straight at Mr. Creeply and the words came tumbling out. "I'm a sheep farmer down in South Australia and when I read in the newspaper that Motte and Bailey had died and left everything to *me*, I came out here to see the old place. My parents brought me once when I was a little girl. I feel really bad that we lost touch but…" She shrugged. "We did. Anyway, I didn't want the Billabong. Not for myself. It's a beautiful place and the sanctuary is great and I wanted it to stay just as it is. I knew if I didn't claim it, it would go to Frank." She shrugged again. "So I came up to see him. I phoned to say when I'd be arriving and someone called Nat Golding answered the phone and came to meet me from the plane. He said he was the new hired hand." She turned to the plum-haired woman. "But he didn't take me to meet Frank. He brought me straight in here and locked me in the tower."

Mr. Creeply sat back heavily. His face had drained even of its natural gray color, and his hands were trembling.

"It's not possible," he croaked. "Here is the birth certificate Miss Barton sent me." He took a folder from the desk drawer. "And letters she's received over the years from the Mr. Bartons…"

"Fakes," said Ida. She was getting agitated. All this was important but she still didn't know where Tod or Frank were. "They've got to be forgeries and fakes."

Mr. Creeply raised his eyes from the desk. "So, who is *this* then?" he asked faintly, staring at the woman with the plum-colored bangs.

"Her name's Avaricia Golding," said Deidre, stepping calmly forward. "But don't feel too bad about it, Mr. Creeply. You're not the first solicitor she's fooled."

"Well, well," said Avaricia. "Not such a drippy little Deidre Dishcloth after all, are you?"

Deidre ignored her and continued talking to Mr. Creeply. "I'm Deidre Chance, International Fraud Squad. I've been on her case for months. She and her brother travel the world cheating heirs out of their inheritance."

Avaricia smiled smugly. "Well, we are an excellent team. Nat's very good with keys and locks and things and I have a Grade A in forgery. I've got the certificate to prove it."

Mr. Creeply's head was reeling. "But why undertake all those dreadful challenges just to get your hands on a wildlife sanctuary in the middle of nowhere?"

Avaricia smiled broadly. "If you don't give me those deeds, Mr. Creeply, you're going to find out. More quickly than you might wish."

Listening just outside the door, Nat took this as his cue. It was time to act. He had been shocked rigid when Ida had run in through the front doorway. He couldn't imagine how she'd got out of the locked room. And he'd been just as shocked when the real Alice and her pet lamb had come hurrying down the stairs. But it didn't matter how they'd escaped. He'd watched and waited, cunningly he thought, and now they were all trapped in the office like fish in a net. He stepped into the doorway. "You tell him, sis," he said. "I'll be back in five."

Avaricia turned and nodded at her brother, still smiling.

Nat disappeared again, slamming and locking the office door behind him. Things might not have gone quite to plan, but he felt in control again.

He glanced up and saw the five sheep who'd got in his way earlier finally coming down again.

If going up a circular staircase had been difficult for the warriors, then coming down was all but impossible and had taken them ages. They tumbled down the last few steps and tottered dazedly out of the tower into the sunshine, looking for Tuftella. They staggered back across the rope bridge, too dizzy to worry about trapping their hooves.

Nat watched them go and resisted the temptation to give them a kick. This was no time for petty revenge. He selected the right key and unlocked the dungeon door. He and Avaricia still had a top card up their sleeves. Two, in fact: they had the old man. And the boy. It was time to use them.

31
The Rowboat

Tod and Frank heard the key turning in the lock. "Let's rush him," said Tod. "We could manage between us."

"Not from here, mate," said Frank. "Not up to our knees in water. Best to keep quiet and stick to plan A."

The door opened and the beam from Nat's flashlight suddenly flooded the dungeon with light. Tod saw for the first time a wooden rowboat bobbing gently in the water on the far side of the dungeon.

"Enjoying your swim?" asked Nat with a smirk.

He pointed a remote control pad at the boat and pressed a button on the keypad.

"See you guys, later," he said from the top of the steps. Then he added with a nasty grunt, "Perhaps."

He slammed the door behind him and locked it, leaving Tod and Frank in darkness again.

"What's that noise?" asked Tod.

They could both hear the quiet, rhythmic beep pulsing somewhere close by.

"Dunno, mate…" said Frank. "I never heard it before."

Tod fumbled in his pocket and pulled out his Eppingham Farm key ring. He didn't have any keys, but he did have a tiny flashlight on it. It wouldn't have dazzled an ant. But he kept it on and splashed toward the noise.

"It's coming from the boat," he said. "Did you know there was a boat here?"

"There's always a rowboat here," replied Frank, rather irritably. "Since the beginning of time. But it's no use if we can't open the portcullis."

Tod was standing beside the boat now. "It's got something in it."

"What?" This was news to Frank.

"And that's what the beeping's coming from."

"Show me."

Tod heard Frank wading through the water toward him. He held his flashlight up and pointed the pathetic little beam down into the boat. It was full of plastic bags, packed tightly together and connected with wires. The beeping seemed to grow louder as Tod and Frank bent to read the print on the bags:

HIGH EXPLOSIVE

WARNING!!!

WILL DETONATE ON CONTACT WITH WATER.

"Walloping Wallabies…" muttered Frank.

Tod swallowed hard. The battery on his tiny flashlight gave up and the light went out.

• • •

Avaricia was enjoying herself in the office.

"You are quite right, Mr. Creeply," she trilled. "Barton's Billabong *is* a pathetic little animal sanctuary in the middle of nowhere. But it also happens to be sitting on this." From her damp pocket, she took a plastic wallet. It contained a map, which she spread on the desk.

"Carbon. Crystallized. You do know what crystallized carbon is?"

"Diamonds?" said a voice from the doorway.

Nat was standing there grinning. At the sight of him, the lamb in the real Alice Barton's arms bleated loudly. It remembered the kicks Nat had given whenever he'd had a chance. She squirmed from her owner's arms and fled.

Alice tried to follow but Nat barred her way.

"It'd be rude to leave before Avaricia's finished talking," he said nastily. And he quietly closed the door.

Avaricia smiled and smoothed the map she had spread on the table. Shelly recognized it as one of the papers she'd seen Deidre studying at Tickler's Turnpike. After Deidre had picked the bag's lock with a bobby pin.

"Everyone knows this whole area is rich in minerals," said Avaricia. "Mostly too deep to be worth extracting. But I just *love* diamonds, so when I saw Mr. Creeply's notice appealing for an heir to this place, I did a bit of digging. In Mr. Creeply's computer files. Hacking, I think they call it. And guess what? I found this old survey map showing a whole lot of lovely crystallized carbon. So I downloaded it."

Mr. Creeply was utterly shocked. "You hacked into the confidential files on my computer? Files I hold on behalf of my clients? How dare you!"

"Oh, I dare anything," replied Avaricia. "Then I had a mineralogist look at the map and he said it was genuine and there's a ninety-nine-point-nine-nine percent chance of finding lovely, lovely diamonds. Right here. And soooo near the surface."

Ida suddenly stamped her foot. "Never mind your diamonds. Where's Frank? Where's my grandson?"

Nat laughed. "We're coming to that in a minute."

"Quite," said Avaricia. "Now, there's only one way to be absolutely certain about the diamonds."

It was Nat's turn again. "So we're going to blow the whole place up and have a look."

"Which, as the rightful legal owner," continued Avaricia, "I now propose to do." Her face hardened as she turned back to Mr. Creeply. "As soon as you hand over the deeds and I *become* the rightful owner."

Mr. Creeply picked up the deed box and clasped it to his chest.

Avaricia smiled. "We do have an insurance policy to *ensure* you hand them over."

She held out her hand for the deeds. "It's called Frank. I believe he's locked in the dungeon with the explosives." She glanced at her brother for confirmation.

Nat gave her a nod. "Yeah, he's still there. And the clock's ticking. Five minutes." He grinned nastily. "Oh—and there's more. The kid's in there too."

32
The Countdown

Down in the dungeon, Frank and Tod were in the water, working on the portcullis wheel again. They had scraped it free of rust but still it wouldn't turn. The beeping was shredding their nerves and they guessed their time was running out.

"Push again…" panted Frank. The wheel shifted a little, then stuck. "And again…"

They pushed, and this time the wheel creaked and ground round almost half a turn. Tod's arms were aching and his feet were going numb in the cold water.

"Once more, Uncle Frank…" Tod braced himself and pushed with all his strength on the wheel.

"She's moving!" cried Frank.

Gradually, as they kept on turning the wheel, the portcullis began to rise. But the beeping was getting faster.

In the office immediately above the dungeon, the tension was becoming unbearable.

"Give her the deeds," the real Alice Barton sobbed. "I don't want the Billabong. I don't want any diamonds. Just give her the deeds and let the old man and the boy go."

Mr. Creeply hesitated. "I c-c-can't." he stuttered. "It would be unethical to give away your rightful inheritance under threat."

"It would be *unethical* to let my grandson die!" shouted Ida. "Please!"

Mr. Creeply's hands were shaking. He clutched the deed box tighter to his chest. "I...I don't know..."

Nat glanced at his watch again, then strode to the desk, leaned across, and grabbed the deed box. "Come on, Avaricia. It's their funeral. We gave them a chance. Let's get out before it goes up."

He turned to the door and grabbed the knob. It came off in his hand.

There was an awful silence.

"Your funeral too, it would appear..." whispered Mr. Creeply .

• • •

In the dungeon, the portcullis was now half open.

"Can you row, Uncle Frank?" panted Tod.

"Never needed to out here in the bush, mate."

"Then you can push." Tod grabbed the side of the wooden rowboat and hauled himself carefully up and over the side. He settled himself as far away from explosives as he could and grasped the oars. "OK, Uncle Frank...Push."

Frank pushed and Tod used the oars to steer the boat toward the open portcullis.

"Steady...steady..." panted Frank. "Don't get water on it..."

"I'm trying..." muttered Tod as the boat lurched forward and out into the lake. The beeping was getting louder and he could now see a digital timer attached to one of the bags. It was counting down. From one hundred and twenty seconds.

Tod grasped the oars more tightly and started to row more strongly, trying hard not to splash. "I can't wait for you, Uncle Frank," he called. "Swim round. Find Gran. Warn her!"

• • •

Inside the office room, pandemonium had broken out. Avaricia was screaming at Nat, who was trying, with shaking hands, to fix the door handle, and Ida and

Shelly were heaving at the bars which covered the small window.

"One minute!" sobbed Nat, on his knees. "One minute!"

"And counting," said Ida stiffly.

• • •

Alice Barton's pet lamb was cowering in the shadows just outside the office door. It had fled from the man with the kicking feet into an even worse dilemma. On the other side of the moat, she could see the crazy Brit sheep. She knew she would feel safe in a flock. Even a flock made up of tourists. But there was the problem of the rope bridge between her and them. She didn't dare step on it.

The warriors were standing in a bemused huddle. They had expected to find Tuftella again somewhere at the bottom of the tower, along with her pale-faced, blond-haired human, but there had been no sign of either. Then Wills suddenly gasped and stared in wonder at something else. A small wooden boat was emerging from right under the tower. An old man was standing waist-deep in the water some way behind it. And sitting in the boat, pulling on the oars, was a boy they all knew well. The boy who brought them cauliflower and cabbage and other nice treats.

"It's Tod," cried Wills.

The Merino lamb had also seen the boat, and with it her chance to get away from the tower without stepping on the rope bridge. She emerged from the shadows and teetered on the edge of the stone rim around the tower.

"And Tuftella!" cried Sal.

Tuftella wobbled for a moment, then hurled herself at the rowing boat and landed with a clack on top of the pile of plastic bags.

Tod flinched and stopped rowing for a moment, shoulders tensed, waiting for an explosion, but nothing happened. The beep went on beeping. Tod ignored the lamb that was now standing bleating agitatedly in front of him and rowed as hard as he could. He had to get the boat as far away from the tower as possible. And then he would have to dive overboard and swim for his life.

The warriors saw their Tuftella's graceful leap and began trotting along the side of the moat after the rowboat.

Forty seconds! Tod dropped the oars and stood up

in the boat. He grabbed the lamb by the scruff of her neck and stuffed her down the front of his shirt. He raised his arms above his head and dived in. It was the split second after his feet left the boat that he saw the crocodile.

33

The Final Thunder

The salty hadn't had a meal for days. Not since a baby wallaby had been foolish enough to step into the creek for a drink. But since then, the local kangaroos and wallabies had learned their lesson and were drinking elsewhere. Hunger, rather than the taste of Oxo's fleece, had driven it to follow the sheep all the way from the creek.

Now it was waddling swiftly and silently toward the moat. It hesitated for a moment. To one side, it could see the little bunch of sheep. Revenge would make its meal taste sweeter. But on the other hand…a boy and a tender lamb would make a nice snack too. And they would be easier to catch. They were in the water, a salty's natural home. It scuttled to the edge of the moat and lowered its head toward the water.

"OhmygrassohmygrassohmyTuftella!" Jaycey's shriek shocked her fellow warriors. Then she shocked them even more by putting her head down and charging at the crocodile. The little horns she was so proud of banged into its scaly hide. The crocodile stopped and turned its head in surprise. Jaycey ran at it again and this time Oxo was with her. His great head whacked into the startled reptile at speed. The long, strong tail lashed furiously but Links was there too now and he caught the very end of it between his teeth. The next moment, he was whipped off his feet as the tail lashed from side to side. But he wouldn't let go.

Jaycey and Wills leapt on to the thick base of the crocodile's tail and jumped up and down, digging their sharp little hooves in as hard as they could. And then Sal clambered up to join them and sat down heavily. The crocodile suddenly found it couldn't move its tail at all. It was really, really angry. Forgetting the boy and the lamb in the water, it reared round to fight off its attackers. But it was difficult to turn completely with all the weight on its tail end and its vicious jaws snapped uselessly on thin air.

Tod thought he must be going mad when he saw the sheep—his and Ida's sheep—attack a crocodile. He swam fast, quickly reached the side of the moat, and hauled himself out. The lamb wriggled from his shirt and ran, bleating pitifully, toward the warriors. It hadn't enjoyed its dunking at all.

Tod paused for a moment, gasping for breath. He shook water from his ears and listened. The bleeps were getting faster and faster. Then they stopped.

"Run!" he yelled. "Oxo, Wills…all of you…Run!"

The warriors had no idea why Tod wanted them to run, but Wills sensed the urgency in the boy's voice. He leapt from the crocodile's tail. "Come on, guys!" he yelled. "Run!"

Without the weight of three large sheep and two lambs on its tail, the crocodile suddenly found itself slipping forward. Its whole body had just slid under the water when the boat exploded.

KER-BOOOOOOM!

Tod and the sheep turned and gazed at the great fountain of water blasting up into the air from the moat.

"Ohmygrass…!" breathed Jaycey. It was the biggest geyser she'd ever seen.

Tuftella was huddling close to Sal's side, whimpering.

"Hush, dear," Sal said soothingly. "You have nothing more to fear. *That* was the final thunder."

• • •

Inside the office the sound of the explosion was ear-splitting. The walls shook, and the neat piles of paper-work cascaded into a chaotic jumble again. Everyone except Ida instinctively crouched low with their hands over their heads. The rumble of the explosion gradually died away and there was a moment's complete silence. Then the handle on the outside of the door suddenly rattled and the door burst open.

"Frank!" Ida, who was still trying to prize the bars from the window, almost threw herself across the room at her brother.

Frank strode in and gave her a quick hug. "It's OK. Tod's safe. Wet but safe. I saw him. And, Ida, you're never going to believe this…"

Ida didn't hear what she would never believe because Deidre had leapt to her feet and was shouting.

"They're getting away. Stop them!"

Nat and Avaricia had been closest to the door when the blast happened. Now they had slipped past Frank and were out of the tower and already making their way across the rope bridge. Shelly jumped up to give chase, but Ida caught her arm and held her back. "I'll do this," she said. She grabbed a paperweight from the desk.

Nat was racing past the animal pens when the heavy glass paperweight whacked him between the shoulder blades and knocked him to the ground.

"Howzat!" yelled Tod from a little way off. "England'll sign you for the second test, Gran."

"Nah," said Uncle Frank, hobbling across the rope bridge. "She's no good with the bat."

The others were all out of the tower now and Shelly was chasing after Avaricia, who was running surprisingly quickly. Maybe it was fear of being caught or maybe all her training on *Destiny* was paying off. She reached the tangerine-orange truck, leapt in, and roared away in a cloud of fumes and dust.

"Holy-moly!" cried Shelly. "You never start that easily for me, Norm. We're gonna have words about this when I get you back."

"Don't worry, dears, she won't get far."

Everyone's attention switched to the new voice.

An elderly, neatly dressed lady, was standing just outside Frank's house. She held up a key.

"I arrived a few minutes ago. And locked the gate behind me."

Ida, Frank, and Tod stared. "Rose!"

34
Crazy Brits

While the family were hugging Rose, Avaricia was trying to drive Norm straight through the locked gate. But he wasn't having any of that sort of treatment and stalled. With a brief backward glance, Avaricia abandoned the truck and climbed shakily over the gate. She was plodding away into the bush when the police roared into sight. They'd narrowly avoided a rather dazed-looking crocodile putting as many miles as it could between itself and Barton's Billabong.

The police picked up Avaricia and locked her and Nat in the tower for safekeeping until they'd worked out what had been going on. Over a cup of tea.

Frank's kitchen had never seen so many people. Rose bustled around smiling and cutting slices from the many delicious cakes she'd brought in her oversized suitcase, and refilling cups.

"Of course, the police didn't believe me when I

phoned from Murkton to say I'd just seen my brother at Barton's Billabong being whacked on the back of the head and dragged away."

"Really?" said Shelly, munching cake. "Shame on them."

"So I caught the first plane out," continued Rose, "and they *had* to listen to me when I turned up on their doorstep."

The policemen exchanged rueful glances. They had indeed had to listen to the angry old English lady who'd marched in and disturbed their peace.

"What are you talking about, Rose?" said Frank. "How did you see Nat bashing me on the head?"

"The webcam," said Rose a touch smugly. "It was still on in your kitchen. So when I Skyped for a chat, I saw it all."

"Go, Auntie Rose," said Tod. "We've got a techno wizard in the family."

Mr. Creeply had retrieved the box of deeds from where Nat dropped them when he was felled by Ida's paperweight, and was again hugging them to his chest. He stood up, pushed his teacup aside, and solemnly handed the box to Alice Barton. The real Alice Barton.

"Dear lady," he said in his quiet, thin voice. "I have

pleasure in handing you the deeds to Barton's Billabong. And I'm"—he sniffed back a tear—"I'm so sorry I almost failed in my duty and gave them to the wrong person."

"Not a problem," said Alice, taking the box. "But don't even think of going yet. I've got another job for you."

"Oh, I couldn't start tidying up all that paperwork again," said Mr. Creeply.

Alice smiled. "No, not that." She slid the box across the table toward Frank. "I want you to transfer the deeds to Barton's Billabong to Frank Smith." She grinned at Frank. "I'm afraid you'll have to spend a bit on repairing the moat, Frank. Sorry about that."

Frank looked down at the box, then slid it gently back across the table. "Forget the moat," he said. "There's something else you should know." He took from his pocket a map very like the one Avaricia had produced in the office. Only dirtier. "Avaricia Golding was quite right. Her mineralogist was too. There *is* a big seam of diamonds under the Billabong. A huge one, in fact."

Even the flies buzzing around the ceiling seemed to go silent.

"Motte and Bailey knew about it years ago," continued Frank. "That's why they bought the land. They knew a mine would destroy this whole wild and beautiful place. So they started their sanctuary, and then they built their tower slap bang on top of the diamonds." He shrugged. "But it would be easy enough to get rid of the tower and get at them."

He looked at Alice and nudged the deed box closer to her. She rested her hands on it for a moment. Everyone had gone very quiet. Alice's pale blue eyes stared back at Frank. Then she pushed the box gently toward him.

"But, Frank, I don't think diamonds suit me."

• • •

Outside the kitchen, the warriors were munching their way through a great pile of hay Tod had brought them.

Tod and Ida had both wept a few secret tears into Oxo's and Sal's and Links's and Jaycey's and Wills's fleeces as they hugged them all. And when they went back to join the tea party in the kitchen, they made sure they sat where they could keep an eye on their little flock through the kitchen window.

"Well, Auntie Rose," said Tod, "I guess we'll never know how they got here. But we're glad they did." He took another large slice of homemade cake. "And you too, of course."

"My little Guinevere seems to have taken a liking to your rare breeds," said Alice. "Especially the Southdown ewe."

"Ah, Sal's very motherly," said Ida. "I expect she's teaching her a thing or two."

Ida didn't know how very right she was.

• • •

"You see, Tuftella, dear, it all began with the Songs of the Fleece. That's how we knew you were in distress and came all this way to find you."

Guinevere couldn't think why they all kept calling her Tuftella. Privately, she still thought they were crazy Brits. But they were nice Brits too, and she did like being close to Sal.

Oxo found a chunk of banana in the hay he was chewing. "Not as good as lotions and potions," he said. "But not bad."

None of the warriors had seen what happened to their fairy godtingy after the explosion in the water. What with the bang and the crocodile and rescuing Tuftella and then seeing Tod and then Ida, their minds had been rather full.

"I think," said Sal suddenly, "we should raise our voices in a chorus of thanks to our fairy godtingy. She has obviously gone because we no longer need her. But without her help, we would not have succeeded. Links...?"

"Erm...?" Links gulped the mouthful of hay he was chewing. "Right...right..."

While Links was rapidly composing the rap Sal had clearly demanded, Wills wondered briefly about how they were to get home again.

• • •

Tod and Ida were wondering that too.

"Not a problem," said Deidre with a smile. "So long as you don't mind a long sea voyage. There's a lady in Britain who's the rightful owner of a beautiful boat called *Destiny*. And she wants it back. Our dear Avaricia cheated her out of her inheritance too." She smiled. "I'm sure Skipper Ed will be happy to take us all."

"Wouldn't mind a peek at damp old Britain myself," said Shelly. "Is the boat big enough to take Norm?"

Then the humans all looked up at the strange sound wafting in through the window.

"How weird..." exclaimed Alice. "My sheep never do that."

"Oh, ours often do," said Ida. Then she added with just a touch of boastful pride. "But they *are* rare breeds."

Outside, the warriors were joining Links in a rousing chorus of his latest composition.

"We's the Warrior Sheep and we is the best,

At rescuin' maidens who is well in distress.

But we had some dramas and we wanna shout,

For our fairy godtingy who helped us out.

An' direction-wise, we gotta say too,

Good on you guys, to those wild kangaroos.

'cause they put us right on the Jumpup Trail,

And that led us on to the scaly tail...

The scaly tail of a fearsome croc,

But he didn't stand a chance 'gainst

A rare breeds flock.

So let's all hear it for the final thunder,

And a high, high hooves to bein' Down Under."

"High hooves!" shouted the warriors.

"Crazy Brits..." muttered Tuftella. But she raised her front hoof and clacked it with the rest. "High hooves!"

Also available from Sourcebooks Jabberwocky

The Quest of the Warrior Sheep
The Warrior Sheep Go West